On Me 'Ead, Santa!

Ten Sensational New Soccer Stories!

Scholastic Children's Books,
Commonwealth House, 1–19 New Oxford Street,
London, WC1A 1NU, UK
a division of Scholastic Ltd
London ~ New York ~ Toronto ~ Sydney ~ Auckland
Mexico City ~ New Delhi ~ Hong Kong

First published in the UK by Scholastic Ltd, 1999

ISBN 0 439 01288 0

Typeset by DP Photosetting, Aylesbury, Bucks
Printed by WSOY, Finland

1 2 3 4 5 6 7 8 9 10

Dear Reader,

Congratulations! You've chosen the finest collection of new football stories around. Ten terrific tales with everything: the goals, the glamour, the glory, the ... hacking! And there's a cunningly cryptic trivia quiz too (look out for the answers after stories two, five, seven and ten). Bet you won't know 'em all! Enjoy, and have a very merry Christmas.

Santa.

Contents

Magic!

Paul Stewart

For Joseph and Anna

Originally I started writing football stories for my son, Joseph. With Brighton and Hove Albion as our local club, he was keen to read about teams which I could make win every time!

If you enjoy *Magic!* and are fanatical about football, then check out the adventures of Gary, Danny and Craig in my FOOTBALL MAD series, available from Scholastic.

"Oh, what?" Vince Mallin exclaimed, as he pulled one of the new shirts from the box. "What's this?"

Their coach, Mr Miller – or "Magic" Miller as he was better known – beamed. "I thought you'd all be pleased," he said. "New shirts for the new cup-winners."

Vince looked at him. "Where did you get them done, sir?"

"That new place on Market Street," came the reply. "Turned out well, haven't they?"

"Almost," said Vince.

Mr Miller frowned. "What do you mean?"

Vince held the shirt up for everyone in the changing room to see. It was red, with a white trim. Across the front was the name of the school: St Mark's Junior School. Above this was a white halo-shaped oval. It should have contained their nickname – The Saints. That was what the halo was all about. Unfortunately, the printer had got it slightly – but crucially – wrong...

"The *Stains*!" Micky Dean exclaimed.

The other team-members read the misprint, and a loud groan went round the changing room. The "t" was definitely in the wrong place.

"Typical," grumbled Jarrod Evans.

"We'll be a laughing stock!" said Jim Bakewell.

"The most important match of the year," said Vince Mallin, "and we look like a joke."

Vince was right. It *was* the most important match of the year.

Q: WHICH ENGLISH PLAYER HOLDS THE RECORD FOR THE MOST PREMIERSHIP HAT-TRICKS IN ONE SEASON?

After playing well all season, St Mark's now faced Kingfisher Middle in the final of the County Cup. The previous year, the same two teams had also played. On that occasion Kingfisher won two-one. The boys of St Mark's were determined that history would not repeat itself.

As he looked round their glum faces, Mr Miller felt awful. He'd tried to boost the team's morale; to make them feel good about themselves – and he'd ended up doing exactly the opposite.

"Come on, lads," he said. "No one will even notice."

"*We* did," said Kev Marshall.

Mr Miller nodded awkwardly. "Yeah, well, I'll get them changed just as soon as I can, but you'll have to play in them today. They're all we've got. Try them on," he said. "See if they fit at least!"

The boys shuffled round, reluctant to do what they were told. Outside, they could hear the crowd cheering and chanting as the kick-off drew nearer. Once the team appeared, and word went round that they were now the Stains, those cheers would turn to jeers – and no one liked to guess what chants might start up.

"It's a bit like when a pigeon does its droppings down your back," Mr Miller was saying. The boys were puzzled. A couple of them turned and looked at their coach as though he was mad. "My gran reckoned it was good luck," he went on. "And why?"

No one said a word.

"Because the bad luck's already happened." From their blank expressions, it was clear that no one had understood. "Look, what I'm saying is this," said Mr Miller. "The misprint on the

Q: WHICH PREMIERSHIP SIDE PLAYS AT PRIDE PARK?

shirts was the bad luck, so now you're due some good luck. You're going to win the match for sure!"

Unconvinced – but with no other choice – the boys removed their school uniform and changed into the football strip. Mr Miller looked round and nodded approvingly.

"Magic!" he said.

Dave Astley, the team captain, smiled to himself. *Magic*. It was Mr Miller's favourite word. He would shout it out encouragingly after every decent pass, header or shot at goal. It was the reason his nickname was "Magic" Miller and not, as some of the new boys imagined, because he had supernatural powers.

"Right then, lads," he said, when everyone was changed. "Listen up."

The team formed a circle around him.

"I don't have to tell you how important this match is," he said. "So I want you all on your best behaviour. Is that understood?" A rumble of assent went round. Mr Miller turned to Vince Mallin. "Nothing silly. All right?"

The St Mark's striker looked down at the floor. Although he was the team's lead goalscorer that season, he had a reputation for being mouthy. Twice in recent matches he'd got yellow cards for arguing with the referee; once he'd been sent off. That couldn't happen today. The final was too important a game to end up playing with ten men.

"All right?" Mr Miller repeated firmly.

"Yes, sir," Vince muttered.

Mr Miller nodded. "Last year saw us beaten by Kingfisher," he reminded the team. "This year we're going to put that matter right. OK?"

Q: CAN YOU NAME ALL THE LEAGUE TEAMS THAT TV PUNDIT "CLEVER" TREVOR BROOKING PLAYED FOR DURING HIS LONG AND ILLUSTRIOUS CAREER?

"Yes," said the boys.

Mr Miller cupped his hand to his ear. "Can't hear you," he said.

"YEAH!" they bellowed.

"That's more like it," said Mr Miller. "Go on, then. Get out there – and win that cup!"

As the two teams walked out on to the pitch, the crowd – a sea of waving red and blue – roared their approval. Dave Astley for St Mark's and Ricky Torrance, the Kingfisher captain, trotted up to the middle of the pitch where the referee was waiting for them.

"New shirts, eh?" said Ricky.

Dave nodded. Even though he went to a different school, Ricky Torrance lived on the same estate as him and Vince. Dave knew he would leap at the chance to take the mickey if he could, and raised his hand to hide the word in the halo. But Ricky had already seen it.

"The *Stains*?" he sneered.

Dave's heart sank. All round him, he heard the rest of the Kingfisher team sniggering and, from the crowd, a chorus of *"When the Stains go marching in"* echoed round the ground. To a player, the St Mark's team wished the ground would simply swallow them up.

Ricky won the toss. Dave sighed. With his own team's morale suddenly at an all-time low, it was going to be an uphill struggle.

The match started off at a measured pace, with both sides playing safe. Then, some fifteen minutes into the game, King-fisher shifted up a gear.

Q: WHY WAS STANLEY MILDON'S 1934 DEBUT FOR HALIFAX NOT EXACTLY THE BEST OF STARTS?

"Come on you Bluebirds," shouted their supporters, sensing an imminent goal. And despite Mr Miller's cries of "Magic!" whenever any of the St Mark's team tried anything halfway decent, it was clear which way the game was going.

Suddenly, in the twenty-third minute, the Kingfisher number eight chipped the ball over to the right wing with just the right amount of backspin. It was picked up by their number five. He hurtled up the line, before passing the ball back to the centre where the number ten – Ricky Torrance, no less – was waiting to receive it just outside the penalty area.

The St Mark's defence was all over the place. Ricky was unmarked.

He took control of the ball, dribbled round the first defender and shot with his left foot. The ball glanced off Jim Bakewell's foot and was deflected, spinning wildly, to the far right. Kev Marshall dived valiantly, but he was never going to get there. The ball thudded into the net. Kingfisher Middle had gone one-nil up.

As they made their way back to the halfway line, Ricky caught Vince's eye. "Bluebirds one," he said, "Stains ... lost!"

"Leave it out, Ricky," said Vince.

"So, you're not worried then?" Ricky taunted. "Not scared of another defeat?"

"No way."

"You know what happened last year..."

"That was last year," said Vince, between gritted teeth. "We're gonna win this year."

Ricky grinned. "That's not what they think," he said, as the Kingfisher supporters' chant echoed round the pitch to the tune of *Amazing Grace*.

Q: WHICH LEEDS AND ENGLAND PLAYER WAS AFFECTIONATELY KNOWN AS THE GIRAFFE?

"Bluebirds, Bluebirds, Bluebirds, Bluebirds. . ."

"Blue *nerds*, more like," Vince snorted. "Or should that be blue *turds*?"

"No, that's you lot," said Ricky.

"You what?" said Vince.

"That's why you're called the Stains – coz of the skid-marks in your pants." He laughed. "I knew you were scared!"

And with that he turned and trotted off. Furious, Vince felt his fists clenching, his face burning. He opened his mouth. . .

"Don't!" came a voice, and a hand gripped his arm. Vince spun round. It was Dave Astley, who had been monitoring everything that was going on. "He's not worth it, Vince."

"But. . ."

"He was just trying to wind you up."

"Yeah, well, he did a good job," said Vince, but his anger had gone.

Dave breathed a sigh of relief. "Don't let him get to you," he said. "This is the final, Vince. You get yourself sent off and we'll lose it for sure."

"Yeah, all right," said Vince irritably. He stomped back up the pitch, taking care to avoid Ricky's taunting stare as he passed him.

The whistle went and the match started up again. There was an edge to it now. St Mark's – keen to equalize – upped their game. And Kingfisher responded. Up and down the pitch the ball went, with one team and then the other, taking possession and driving forwards – only to be denied a shot at goal right at the last moment.

Then, in the fortieth minute, the Kingfisher number five received a yellow card for bringing Jarrod Evans down. Jim

Q: WHO IS THE OLDEST PLAYER TO HAVE SCORED IN THE WORLD CUP FINALS?

Bakewell moved up to take the free kick. He tapped it to Dave Astley, who punted it back to Jarrod, racing up through midfield.

Jarrod trapped the ball deftly, tapped it forwards and – *BOOF!* – struck it with the inside of his right foot. The kick was a beaut. It soared up into the air, and was still rising as it whistled past their goalie's outstretched fingers and slammed into the back of the net.

"YEAH!" The St Mark's supporters roared with delight.

A moment later they realized something was wrong. The ref hadn't given the goal. He ran over to speak to his assistant on the right touchline.

"What's going on?" Jarrod was asking anyone who would listen.

The referee turned round. He wagged his arm from side to side. It was no goal.

The St Mark's team raced across to the referee and surrounded him. Why had the goal been disallowed? they demanded to know. Why?

The referee turned to Dave Astley. "Your number nine was offside," he said.

"*Me?*" Vince yelled. "Me, offside?"

"When the ball was struck," said the referee.

"I was not!" he yelled. "And anyway, I didn't affect the play. I was nowhere near."

The referee shrugged and turned away.

"Oy, did you hear me?" Vince yelled.

Dave and Jarrod grabbed him by the arms, one on either side, and frog-marched him away. "Leave it," said Dave.

"Yeah, if anyone should be miffed, it's me," said Jarrod.

Q: CAN YOU NAME THE FIRST ENGLISH DOUBLE-WINNING SIDE?

"But not with me!" Vince shouted. "A situation like that, the ref's supposed to use his discretion. No way did I interfere with play. No way…" He tore himself free and spun round. "Where's your white stick," he shouted, "you cheating, pigging—"

The referee stopped and turned slowly to face him. He beckoned. His hand went for his back pocket. Dave Astley groaned. What was it to be. A yellow card – or a red one? If Vince was sent off they might as well give up now.

Taking his time, the referee sorted through the cards, selected one, and held it up.

Yellow! It was yellow.

"Thank heavens for that," Dave muttered to himself. Vince was being given a second chance.

The closing minutes of the first-half ticked past. It was a worrying time for Dave Astley. Buoyant after the disallowed goal, Kingfisher were pressing harder than ever, while his own team – dismayed at having their equalizer snatched away so cruelly – were finding it hard to put up an effective opposition.

Nor was the situation being helped by Ricky Torrance. Needling Vince at every opportunity, he was testing the St Mark's striker to breaking point. To his credit, Vince managed not to rise to the bait, but the longer they played, the more likely he was to lose his temper.

In the forty-fourth minute he did just that. He and Ricky had been battling it out for the ball over by the line until Ricky – or so he claimed – kicked it off Vince's inside-heel and out of play. As the ball bounced away, both boys appealed for the throw-in.

"It went right between my legs," Vince protested.

"Rubbish," said Ricky. "It came off you."

 **Q:** BY WHAT NICKNAME WERE ENGLAND'S 1966 WORLD CUP WINNING SIDE BETTER KNOWN?

"It pigging did not!" Vince shouted.

Ricky smirked as Kingfisher were awarded the throw-in. "Typical," he muttered. "No sense, no feeling. Just like a *stain*."

The referee strode purposefully towards them. Sensing a possible second yellow card, the Kingfisher supporters tried their best to influence his decision. "Off! Off! Off!" they roared.

"One more incident like that and you *are* off," the ref warned Vince. "All right?"

Vince nodded, smarting at the unfairness of it all.

For the second time, the St Mark's team breathed a sigh of relief. They'd been let off the hook again. Yet, as play resumed, they were all wondering to themselves why Magic Miller didn't substitute Vince now, while he still could. Surely it was only a matter of time before he got himself sent off.

Finally, the referee blew for the end of the first half. At last! Dave and his team had never before been so pleased to hear the sound of the whistle.

Mr Miller walked on to the pitch with a trayful of quartered oranges, looking surprisingly untroubled.

"You're doing fine," he said. "OK, so we're one-nil down, but it's nothing to get in a sweat about. Your passing's sound. You're making the best of your opportunities. And that was a fantastic goal, Jarrod. Magic! It was unfortunate it was disallowed…"

The team muttered ominously.

"But disallowed it was," Mr Miller went on. "There's no point fretting over what could have been or should have been. Just go out there and make sure the next goal you score counts. All right?" He clapped his hands together. "Magic!"

Q: WHO WAS THE FIRST PLAYER TO BE SENT OFF IN AN FA CUP FINAL?

The boys nodded but the Saints – or the Stains, as the chanting crowd kept reminding them – were feeling anything but magic.

"Mark your man, stay tight and keep your shape," he told them, as he collected up the orange peel. "Now, go on. If you give it your best shot I guarantee that in forty-five minutes the County Cup will be ours!"

Buoyed up by their coach's words of encouragement, the boys set off towards the opposite end of the pitch. As they were leaving, Mr Miller called Vince back. Dave hung round to hear what he was about to tell him.

"As for you, Vince," he said.

Vince looked away. "I wasn't offside," he muttered. "I—"

"When are you going to learn?" Mr Miller interrupted sharply. "The referee's word is final. Argue, and you make things worse. And not only for you, but for the whole team." He paused. "Do you want to win the final this year?"

"Of course I do," said Vince, still staring down at his feet. "But..."

"Then act as if you do," said Mr Miller. "And look at me when I'm talking to you!"

Vince turned round. Mr Miller looked sternly into the boy's eyes. Dave watched them both with interest. It wasn't often that Vince Mallin looked so sheepish. Mr Miller's brow knitted; his eyes glinted.

"You will be quiet throughout the second half," he said. "You will not utter a single word of dissent, either to another player or to the referee. You will say nothing till the final whistle. Do you understand me?"

 **Q:** WHICH PREMIERSHIP SIDE ARE NICKNAMED THE TOFFEES?

Vince nodded and swallowed nervously. "Yes, sir," he whispered.

Dave groaned. He knew Vince. So far as he was concerned, it would still be better to substitute him before he could land St Mark's in any more trouble.

It was a different team which kicked off at the beginning of the second half. Suddenly, St Mark's were working together, sure-footed and accurate and, urged on by their supporters, they dominated the play.

Eight minutes later they were rewarded with that elusive equalizer when a quickly taken free kick resulted in a perfect one-two manoeuvre and a fantastic goal by Pete West.

"YEAH!" roared the crowd.

"Magic!" shouted Mr Miller from the sideline.

"But it's not over yet," Ricky snarled at Vince as they trotted back up the pitch for the Kingfisher kick-off. "We're not going to get beaten by a bunch of stinky stains!"

Vince turned on him.

"Pure magic!" Mr Miller shouted.

Vince closed his mouth, and turned away.

The match got underway again. Fast and furious it was, with both teams playing to the best of their ability. Passing, heading, dribbling, tackling – it was all text-book stuff. The crowd bellowed their appreciation. In the fifty-seventh minute, the Kingfisher goalie got a hand to Vince's devastating shot from the corner of the penalty box. Ten minutes later, Kev Marshall's spectacular dive prevented Ricky Torrance putting Kingfisher two-one up. With twenty minutes to go, it was still anyone's game.

Q: WHICH CLUB MAKE THEIR HOME AT THE DELL?

"Come on you Saints," Dave shouted as they thundered back up the pitch. "We can do it."

He tapped the ball across to Jarrod, who kicked it back. Vince ran up ahead, taking care not to get stranded offside. A gap in the defence opened up. Dave punted the ball up the field. Vince gathered it neatly and dribbled past his marker. Their number two made a dash for him but Vince kept his cool. He nutmegged the defender and, sprinting now, made a run at the goal.

Faster and faster, he ran. The ball seemed glued to his feet. He glanced up to see the goalie hopping about from foot to foot, uncertain whether to stay his ground or rush out. Over the penalty line Vince went and...

"*Aaaargh!*" he screamed.

Scythed down from behind by their number two, Vince tumbled to the ground and rolled over and over. There was pain in his shin – agonizing pain. The whistle blew. He looked round expectantly. A penalty. It had to be a penalty.

But, no! The referee had done it to him again! There he was, standing behind him, pointing to a spot *outside* the penalty area and calling for a free kick!

Vince, still nursing his throbbing shin, looked up and yelled.

"It was a pigging penalty, you blind cretin!"

At least, that was what he intended to yell – but although his lips moved, no sound emerged. He tried again. Dave Astley watched, horrified that Vince was finally going to get himself sent off. But when Vince tried, a third time, to let the ref know exactly what he thought – of his decision, his eyesight, his intelligence – his voice was still little more than a husky squeak.

Q: WHO WAS THE FIRST ENGLISH-BASED FOREIGN PLAYER TO SCORE A GOAL IN A WORLD CUP FINAL?

"Are you OK?" Dave asked, as he jogged over to help him up.

Vince looked at him. "Khhh," he said, nodding. He climbed to his feet and stepped forward tentatively on his injured leg. It held up. He grabbed Dave by the arm. "Khhoiss khhonhh," he rasped.

"Your voice has gone?" said Dave. "Just as well, mate. We'd be down to ten men if it hadn't."

The free kick was taken, but wasted. St Mark's lost possession. And with everything left to play for and only quarter of an hour remaining till the final whistle, they couldn't afford to be sloppy. A draw would mean deciding the match on penalties, and no one wanted that.

Five minutes later, Vince was back. Racing in to intercept a careless pass, he took possession of the ball and sped back up the pitch towards the opposition goal. This time he took no chances. As the goalie rushed towards him, he kicked the ball firmly. It was a punishing shot that curled over the goalie's outstretched fingers and landed with a devasting *thwack* in the back of the net.

Two-one. The St Mark's supporters went wild; a whooping, cheering sea of red.

"Magic!" yelled Mr Miller. "Magic!"

On the pitch, the compliments from the rest of the team came thick and fast. Usually, Vince was not one to be backward in blowing his own trumpet, but for once he made no attempt to tell everyone how brilliant he'd been. He simply couldn't.

Dave glanced round at Mr Miller who was still standing on the line, clapping and cheering. Could *he* have something to do with Vince's mysterious silence? he wondered. He remembered how the coach's brows had knitted; how his eyes had glinted. *You will*

Q: WHO HOLDS THE RECORD FOR THE MOST PENALTIES SCORED IN AN ENGLISH LEAGUE SEASON?

be quiet throughout the second half, he'd told him. *You will say nothing till the final whistle.*

Still, with only twelve minutes of play left – plus a bit of injury time – he couldn't think about that now. They had to stay calm, to maintain possession, to shut down any attempt at goal...

And that was what they did. Calm, cool, ruthlessly efficient, the St Mark's team ran rings round the opposition. Not only were they holding on to their lead, but it was looking increasingly likely that they might even double it.

The crowd started singing again, this time with the proper words: "*Oh, when the Saints, go marching in...*"

In the eighty-eighth minute, a stinging shot at goal from Jarrod Evans was tipped over the crossbar by the goalie. It was a corner. Taking it quickly, Vince floated the ball over to the far post.

Ricky Torrance leaped up to head it away. But Jarrod leaped higher, and nodded the ball down. It bounced over the line and into the net. He'd scored – making up for the disallowed goal earlier in the match and bringing the score to three-one.

"MAGIC!" Mr Miller roared.

The next moment, three whistle-blasts echoed round the pitch. It was all over. They'd won!

Dave ran over to Vince and clapped him on the back. "Fantastic corner!" he said.

"Pigging brilliant, weren't it!" said Vince, and his hand shot to his mouth. "I can talk again!"

Mr Miller ran on to the pitch and came over to congratulate them. "Magic!" he said. "A magic performance." He winked. "Didn't I tell you that getting the name wrong would bring you

Q: WHO WAS THE FIRST PLAYER TO SCORE MORE THAN 100 GOALS IN BOTH ENGLISH AND SCOTTISH TOP-FLIGHT SOCCER?

good luck? I'm proud of you. All of you." He turned to Vince. "And especially you, lad – for finally managing to control that tongue of yours."

Vince nodded, but didn't explain what had happened. After all, what *had* happened? Why had he been struck dumb? Forty-five minute laryngitis? It made no sense.

As Mr Miller went to congratulate the others, Dave and Vince turned to one another.

"*Magic* Miller," said Vince. "Do you think he really is?"

Dave shrugged. "I dunno," he said. "Maybe he hypnotized you. Or maybe you just lost your voice coz of all the tension and that. I haven't got a clue." He grinned. "But I'll tell you what. We've just won the County Cup for the first time ever. That's what I call magic!"

The Lift

Chris d'Lacey

For Blair

I love football. Always have. Pity I look like a lanky stick of rhubarb in footy shorts, but there you go. I once missed a sitter from six yards out in a crucial semi. Fiona Flightley was passing at the time...

I loved Subbuteo when I was a kid, and you can read all about it in *The Table Football League*, available from Scholastic. Oops, there's the whistle. Gotta go...

"If we can keep their forwards quiet," said Glen. "I reckon we've got a real chance."

"Course we have," Kevin Potter declared, writing his name (in vanilla ice cream) on the window of the bus shelter. "We're gonna whup 'em, I say. DEN-BY! DEN-BY! ALL THE WAY TO WEMBLEY!" He flung his arms (and his ice cream) into the air. The cornet soared into the middle of the road and was instantly splatted by a passing lorry.

Glen shook his head and sighed. "Kev, you've gotta be a *bit* realistic. We're not gonna 'whup' a team that are second in the Premier League. Cranford United are practically in Europe; *we* might make the play-offs for Division Three – if we're lucky."

"It's the cup, though, isn't it?" Kevin said, flashing an optimistic grin. "Anything can happen in the cup, can't it? You heard what Dad said yesterday: big teams are frightened of an underdog – especially a team in form, like Denby. We're giant-killers. *And* we've got home advantage."

Glen nodded. He couldn't argue with that. Lots of good teams had come to grief in the pressure-cooker atmosphere of Denby Dale. But Cranford United were better than good. They had nine internationals in their squad, including—

"Bus is coming," Kevin announced. He walked to the kerb and stuck out his hand. The number eighteen came trundling forwards, brushing the branches of the sycamore trees.

Q: WHICH PLAYER HOLDS THE WORLD RECORD FOR THE QUICKEST EVER HAT-TRICK?

Glen pushed back the blue and white scarf around his wrist. It was 2:25 on his Simpsons watch. On a normal match day they would reach Denby Dale in about twenty minutes. But the traffic in town would be bad this afternoon. The papers were reporting a sell-out crowd. Eighteen thousand people descending on the tiny Denby ground. Eighteen *thousand*. It sounded like the whole of the town itself.

"Have you got the right change?" Kevin asked suddenly.

"Uh?" went Glen, still lost in thoughts of crowd estimations.

Have you got the right mon-ey? Kevin repeated – but this time not in words. Instead he made signs with his fingers and hands.

Glen frowned thoughtfully, interpreting the movements. *Yes*, he signed back, and produced a handful of coins as evidence.

Kevin gave him a big thumbs-up.

Glen smiled and counted out the fares. If anyone had told him a year ago he'd be able to talk without moving his lips, he would have just laughed them right in the face. But that was before the accident, of course. A year was a long time in anyone's life – particularly Kevin Potter's.

Suddenly, Kevin yelped and jumped away from the kerb. Glen looked up. A sleek-looking car had just cut quickly in front of the bus and screeched to a halt underneath Kevin's arm.

"Oh no, I think I've hailed a taxi," Kevin said.

Glen ran his eye over the car. It didn't look much like a taxi to him. It was long and silver with pop-up headlights and a sporty frame. A smoky-coloured window scrolled smoothly down.

"Oi, you pair," a man's voice said.

Glen and Kevin exchanged a glance.

"Do you think he means us?" Kevin whispered.

 **Q:** WHICH ENGLISH LEAGUE SIDE ARE KNOWN AS THE BAGGIES?

Glen shrugged. He had one eye glued to the bus. It had wheezed to a halt a few yards from the stop. The driver was looking distinctly annoyed at the sight of a car parked in a lane marked BUSES ONLY. He pipped his horn and flashed his lights.

The man in the car took no notice. "Down here," he shouted, leaning over. Glen crouched a little to peer into the car. The man looked about thirty and had short-cropped, bleached-white, curly hair. He was wearing sunglasses and a casual suit. An impressive-looking sports bag was taking up most of the passenger seat.

"What do you want?" Glen asked. It seemed impolite not to answer the man, even though his manner was brusque and arrogant. But the bus wasn't going to hang around for ever. If they missed it, they'd miss the first half of the game.

"You going to the football?" the man enquired.

"Yes," said Glen, flapping his scarf. He had a feeling he recognized the driver from somewhere, but he couldn't quite place him from this strange angle. From the corner of his eye he noticed Kevin tilting for a look as well.

"Do you know where the stadium is?"

"Stadium?" said Kevin, wrinkling his nose.

"We know where Denby Town play," said Glen.

"Good," said the man, spitting a piece of gum into his hand. He flicked it through the passenger window. It rebounded off the shelter with a bullet-like splat. "Get in. You can direct me to it."

Kevin and Glen exchanged another glance. Before either could respond, the bus driver pipped his horn again.

Q: WHO WAS THE FIRST ENGLISH PLAYER TO BE SENT OFF IN THE WORLD CUP FINALS?

The man in the car muttered something rude. He got out, pushed his sunglasses into his hair and rapped a knuckle on the bus driver's window. "Do you know who I am?" he demanded.

The bus driver merely threw up his hands. He didn't appear to recognize the smartly-dressed figure. But Glen and Kevin did.

"Wow! It's Graeme Shooter!" gasped Kevin.

Glen's mouth fell open in shock.

Graeme Shooter? The Cranford United and England striker? Offering them a lift to Denby Dale? It had to be a dream, surely?

Not for the driver of the Eighteen bus.

"You can't park there," he grumbled, pushing his window open a crack.

Graeme Shooter pointed to his chest. "I can park where I like, *mate*."

The bus driver slammed his window shut and hastily unbuttoned a pocket of his uniform. Glen wondered for an idle moment if Graeme Shooter was about to get a yellow card. But the bus driver merely took out a pad, squinted fiercely at the England man's car and jotted down his registration.

Graeme Shooter seemed unconcerned. He strutted back to his car again and shot the awestruck boys a chiselled glance. "Stand there much longer and you'll take root," he growled. "Doors're open. Get in the back."

"Smart!" cried Kevin and made a move forward.

Glen reached out and held him back. "Erm, sorry, Mr Shooter. We're not supposed to accept lifts with ... strange men."

Graeme Shooter stuck his chin in the air. "Are you for real or what? I'm not a strange man. I'm Graeme Shooter. Footballing superstar. Face on a zillion football mags."

 **Q:** WHICH TWO ITALIAN GIANTS SHARE THE SAN SIRO?

"And mugs," beamed Kevin.

"You what?" the footballing superstar snapped.

"I've got your picture on a mug, Mr Shooter."

Graeme Shooter rippled his impressive shoulders. "You'll be the mug if you don't get in this car." He jerked a thumb behind him. "If I'm not mistaken, there goes your bus." He gestured at the driver as the bus slipped past. "Now, are you showing me this Denby dump or not?"

Kevin looked excitedly at Glen. "Come on," he hissed. "*Graeme Shooter*. We can get his autograph. We can touch his boots."

Glen gave a reluctant nod. Kev was right. A lift with an England player did seem far too good to miss, even if he had called Denby a dump. Glen opened the door.

Leopard-skin seat covers. Graeme Shooter had leopard-skin seat covers. And a nodding dog. And furry dice. And a cassette of Country & Western hits. Glen prayed he wouldn't puke.

Meanwhile, Kevin was in the car, gibbering with excitement and giving out directions: "Just follow that bus, Mr Shooter," he said, pointing at the dwindling Number Eighteen. "That goes right past the Denby ground."

"I'm not following a *bus*," said Graeme Shooter, slipping a comb through his tightly-permed hair. "This is a mark one Venus Volcano. It does nought to sixty in under five seconds. Ever wondered what it's like when the space shuttle takes off?"

"Space *shutt…le*?" went the boys as the Venus Volcano roared up the road, leaving their stomachs behind at the bus stop. Glen thought he heard a screech of brakes somewhere. Graeme Shooter didn't even look in his mirror.

 **Q:** WHO IS THE WORLD'S TOP PROFESSIONAL GOALSCORER OF ALL TIME?

"Right," he said, as the car zipped effortlessly past the bus. "Which way are we going?"

"Head for the signs saying 'Town'," said Glen, wishing Graeme Shooter would slow down a bit. They had just whizzed past an old man on a bike, almost blowing him into the gutter.

"Town?" said the striker, buckling a lip. "I don't want to get stuck in a load of traffic. What about this ring-road exit to the right?" He pointed to the sign as they approached a roundabout.

"That's the long way round," said Glen, remembering that his dad had tried it once.

"Not in this car," Graeme Shooter sniffed and swept across to the right hand lane. Ten seconds later they were on a dual carriageway, cruising at ninety miles per hour. "That's better," the Cranford superstar said, and popped a stick of chewing gum into his mouth.

"Mr Shooter, can I ask you a question?" said Kevin.

"If you must," Graeme Shooter replied.

Kevin bristled with delight. He beamed at Glen then asked his question: "Why do footballers, y'know, chew chewy all the time?"

Glen sighed and pressed a hand to his brow. He realized Kevin was a bit starstruck, but honestly – what a thing to ask!

The England centre forward took the question in his stride. "Looks good on the telly," he said.

"Wow," went Kevin, totally gobsmacked.

Graeme Shooter pursed his lips. "Makes you look professional in front of the cameras."

"Ace," said Kevin. "I'm gonna chew some chewy in our next school match!"

Q: WHICH SIDE ARE NICKNAMED THE RED DEVILS?

"Don't be dumb," Glen tutted. "You'll get detention. Anyway, when do *we* ever get on a camera?"

Something flashed at the side of the road.

"What was that?" said Glen.

"Speed camera," Graeme Shooter sniffed. "I'll get fined a hundred quid now for driving too fast."

"A HUNDRED QUID!" Kevin nearly gagged. "Cor, that's *tons* of dosh."

"Not when you're worth fourteen million on the transfer market," Graeme Shooter said.

"Wow," gasped Kevin. He looked across at Glen. Glen signed a terse response.

Graeme Shooter caught the movement in the corner of his eye. "What's he doing?" he said.

Kevin started to snigger. "He just called you a big head," he snitched.

"Shut up," hissed Glen, going red in the face. He gave Kevin a kick on the ankle.

"He used sign language," Kevin explained. "My dad's going deaf, Mr Shooter. I'm learning signing so I'll still be able to talk to him. Glen's doing it as well – to help me learn faster. Do you want us to teach you some?"

"I know all the signs I need to," the striker replied.

Yeah, thought Glen. He'd seen both of them on Match of the Day last week.

Unruffled, Kevin popped another question: "What's it like when you play for England, Mr Shooter?"

Graeme Shooter jiggled the knot of his tie. "Best feeling in the world," he said.

 Q: WHO IS ENGLAND'S OLDEST EVER INTERNATIONAL DEBUTANT?

"Knew it," Kevin said, rocking in his seat. "Do you think you'll get picked again one day?"

The Venus Volcano screeched to a halt. "Look, I've had hamstring trouble, that's all."

"Err, I don't think you're allowed to stop here!" Glen squeaked, twisting in his seat to check the traffic. A horn-blaring lorry swerved violently past.

"I was rested, not dropped," Graeme Shooter continued, slamming the car back into gear, "and I didn't fall out with the England manager – mind you, he couldn't pick his nose, never mind a decent team. Neither have I lost a yard of pace or my appetite in front of goal. And I was NOT in that night club with one of the Space Gurls, no matter what the papers say."

"We believe you," Kevin said. "If me and Glen were the England managers we'd pick you every game – wouldn't we, Glen?"

Glen wasn't so sure he would. He'd never been a big Graeme Shooter fan, and now he'd met the England player his opinion hadn't changed that much. Graeme Shooter might be a top professional, but that didn't grant him the right to be mean. Glen wondered what Kevin's dad would say if he was getting a lift in this car. But that wasn't possible. Not for a while. Glen shoved the thought to the back of his mind.

"Where *is* this ground?" Graeme Shooter piped.

"Told you it was a long way round," Glen muttered. He checked his watch again. There were now just twenty minutes to kick off. If only they'd taken the route through town.

"Mr Shooter?" said Kevin.

Q: WHO WERE THE LAST FA CUP HOLDERS TO BE KNOCKED OUT BY NON-LEAGUE OPPOSITION?

"What *now?*" the Cranford superstar snapped. "You're worse than a jumping record."

Kevin looked a little wounded, but he let the dig past. "What's the best goal you've ever scored?"

Graeme Shooter tugged his earring. "Too many to choose from, lad."

Glen tutted loudly at that. He disliked Graeme Shooter more by the second. Part of him was even beginning to wish they wouldn't make it to the ground at all. At least then Graeme Shooter couldn't show off even more by scoring the winning goal or something.

"I know which!" Kevin blurted cheerfully. "That header against San Marino in the Euro qualifiers."

Graeme Shooter nodded. "Shall I talk you through it?"

"Brill!" went Kevin.

"No thanks," Glen yawned.

Graeme Shooter talked them through it – conveniently forgetting to mention the fact that he'd not only fouled the San Marino defender but that the referee hadn't noticed his assistant madly flagging the striker offside.

"It's all about positional play," he wallowed. "The key to being me, Graeme Shooter, is to know EXACTLY where you are at all times..."

I wish *I* knew where I was, thought Glen, desperately looking out for a landmark. He checked his watch again. Eighteen minutes. This could be close.

"Do you know what they call me on the Continent, lads?"

Kevin gave a shrug. "Graeme?" he guessed.

Graeme Shooter shook his head. "I'm known as 'Le Moth'."

 **Q:** WHO WAS BRITAIN'S FIRST MILLION POUND PLAYER?

"*Loudmouth?*" said Kevin, not hearing it right. Glen coughed into his fist. In his opinion, 'loudmouth' described Graeme Shooter perfectly.

The striker's response was loud all right: "NO, YOU NUMBSKULL; they call me *The Moth*, because I flutter uncertainly round the goalmouth."

"Oh," said Kevin, thinking about it. "We call them goal-hangers, don't we, Glen?"

"Yeah," said Glen, bursting out laughing.

"Where's this stadium?" Graeme Shooter said harshly, quickly changing the subject. When no one answered, he turned on the radio.

And continuing our tour of the third round ties, we move next to Denby Dale, where lowly Denby Town entertain the mighty Cranford United.

"Den-by!" Kevin chanted.

"Button it," Graeme Shooter warned.

"We're gonna whup you, Mr Shooter," Kevin jeered, whirling his scarf around his wrist.

"With me in the side?" Graeme Shooter gloated. "Listen, lad, I could play with ten *Subbuteo* men and still run rings round your no-hopers."

"We've got a brilliant new centre-back," Glen said tautly, but his words were drowned out by the crackle of the radio.

Late team news. Cranford manager Marcus McFadden has announced that enigmatic striker Graeme Shooter faces a last minute fitness test...

Graeme Shooter roared with laughter.

"Huh! Are you injured?" Kevin gasped. He looked wide-eyed

Q: HOW MANY LEAGUE TITLES DID ERIC CANTONA WIN DURING HIS SIX SEASONS IN ENGLISH FOOTBALL?

at Glen. Glen's mind began to race: if Shooter was out of the Cranford team, Denby's chances were dramatically improved. But Graeme Shooter wasn't acting like a man who expected to be missing a third round cup tie. And his next little outburst proved it.

"No, you dipstick. That's just an excuse. They say I'm facing a fitness test whenever I'm late arriving at the ground. Are you daft as well as deaf?"

There was silence in the back of the car.

"I'm not deaf," Kevin muttered, looking hurt. As if to prove it, he stared at the radio. The pre-match report continued.

And sadly for Denby their promising young centre-back, Aaron Gudabe, has failed to shake off a viral infection...

"Aw no!" went Glen, grabbing chunks of his hair. Without Aaron Gudabe they had no hope of stifling Loudmouth Shooter. Their chances had swung the other way entirely. And Graeme Shooter was revelling in it.

"Looks like a hat-trick for me," he bragged. "He isn't up to much, your centre half, if he can't shake off a measly infection."

There was silence in the back of the car again. Kevin lowered his head and picked at his nails. Glen knew exactly what Kevin was thinking. His mate was back in ward fourteen, Denby General Hospital. They had both been there the night before – visiting Kevin's dad.

Mr Potter was in hospital for "remedial surgery".

Tinkering with the lugs was how he described it. But everyone knew he was playing things down. What "tinkering" really meant was "a delicate operation on the inner ear". A touch and go process that might restore a fraction of Mr Potter's hearing or

Q: AT WHICH EAST ANGLIAN CLUB WOULD YOU FIND THE CANARIES?

leave him profoundly deaf for good. One of the impediments to the success of the procedure was the risk of severe and recurrent infection. There was nothing "measly" about Mr Potter's condition or the effect it was having on Kevin. On the steps outside the hospital, having kissed his dad goodbye, he had broken down and wept so hard that Glen had had to run back and call a nurse. They had taken Kevin back to his dad. Mr Potter had hugged him and told him he was daft. "You know what you need, Kevin," he'd said. "You need a lift. A bit of a tonic. Get along to Denby tomorrow and watch us knock Cranford out of the Cup. That'll stop you worrying about my flaps."

The prescription had been working perfectly as well – until Graeme Shooter had happened along and stirred up all the suffering again. Glen decided something should be said.

"You shouldn't talk about infections like that, Mr Shooter. Kevin's dad got his deafness from an ear infection. It started after he was hit on the head when he was at a football match."

Graeme Shooter eyed Kevin in his rear-view mirror. "Bit of a hooligan, is he, your dad?"

"No!" Kevin shouted, fury on his face. His high opinion of the England striker seemed to have taken a sudden dive. Before Glen could calm him down, Kevin was blurting out the rest of the story. "He was sitting near the touchline at a game last year when someone whacked the ball really hard into the crowd. My dad turned sideways to avoid it, but the ball hit him on the ear and knocked him out. He got an infection after that and now he's in hospital and losing his hearing. And it's not just that. He has trouble remembering things too, sometimes."

Q: WHICH MANAGER FAMOUSLY SAID: "IF GOD HAD MEANT FOOTBALL TO BE PLAYED IN THE AIR HE'D HAVE PUT GRASS ON THE CLOUDS."?

Graeme Shooter picked up a mobile phone. "Well he won't forget this afternoon's game in a hurry. No one forgets a ten-nil drubbing. Now shut up a minute. I need to make a call." He quickly dialled a number with the thumb of one hand.

"You shut up!" Kevin yelled tearfully, slamming a hand into Graeme Shooter's seat.

"Pack that in!" the striker shouted.

"Kev, don't," Glen appealed, gripping Kevin's arm.

"I want to get out!" Kevin demanded. "I don't care how good at footy he is. He shouldn't say bad things about my dad!"

Glen nodded grimly. Someone ought to teach Graeme Shooter a lesson. The Moth had definitely gone too far.

"Yo, Boss! It's me, Shooty!" the striker babbled into his mobile phone. At the same moment the car flashed past a fork in the road that would have taken them to Denby Dale in minutes. Glen grimaced and made a fist. That was it. Time to get even. He nudged Kevin's ankle and sent him a sign.

Stay cool, it said.

"Why?" Kevin pouted.

I'm going to stuff him, Glen replied.

"Yeah, yeah, five minutes," Graeme Shooter barked, clamping the mobile phone to his shoulder. "Boss, don't get your laces knotted. They're only third division rubbish. Whadd'ya mean you're gonna fine me two week's wages? I'm getting directions. I'll be there in a flash." He threw the phone down. "Prat," he mumbled. "Come on, you pair, where's this ground? We must be close by now."

Glen studied the road signs carefully. "We are," he said, "but you missed the turn about half a mile back."

 **Q:** WHICH SCOTTISH SIDE PLAY THEIR HOME MATCHES AT THE UNFORTUNATELY NAMED BOGHEAD PARK?

"Drat," went Graeme Shooter, giving his furry dice a punch. "Can't do a U-ey here, either."

"It's all right," said Glen. "Turn left at those traffic lights up ahead. Then follow the road round as far as it goes. Denby's about ... two miles, I think."

A puzzled frown appeared on Kevin's face. He had a long look out of the rear window.

"Better had be," Graeme Shooter complained, pulling the steering wheel through his hands. "This is a pretty late fitness test, even by my standards. It's gonna cost me near on sixty grand if I don't get to this ground on time."

"That's a lot of money," Kevin said to Glen.

"More than you could dream of," Graeme Shooter muttered.

Glen bit his lip and looked Kevin in the eye. Kevin grinned like a fox and sat forward in his seat. "You can see the floodlights if you look, Mr Shooty." He pointed up the road. Two metal structures came into view, craning over the roof of a tiered stand. "That's where we're going, isn't it, Glen?"

Glen smiled and gave him a thumbs up sign.

Graeme Shooter sighed with relief. "Wonders'll never cease," he muttered, and pressed down hard on the pedal again.

They had travelled in silence for the best part of a minute when the Cranford superstar spoke again. "Big crowd," he remarked, as they started to flash past groups of people, all walking towards the ground.

"We always get loads up here," said Kevin. He flapped his scarf and grinned at Glen.

"Why are they in yellow and black?" said Graeme Shooter. "I thought your lot played in blue?"

Q: AT WHAT CLUB MIGHT YOU SEE FANS WAVING AN INFLATABLE HADDOCK CALLED HARRY?

"That's our away strip," Glen explained. "Cranford play in blue-striped shirts."

"But you're at home," Graeme Shooter said. "We're the ones who are s'posed to change."

"It said in the paper," Kevin interrupted calmly, "that our manager thought we ought to change because you look so cool in your strip, Mr Shooty."

"Huh. Trying to put us off more like," said the striker. "I've never played a team of bumblebees before."

Suddenly, he blared his horn. The crowds and the traffic had swelled so much that the Venus Volcano had slowed to a crawl. Graeme Shooter lowered a window. "Get out of the fizzing way!" he shouted. A large section of the crowd turned their heads.

"Cor, it's Graeme Shooter!" a pair of boys gasped. A crowd of supporters pressed towards the car.

Can I have your autograph please, Mr Shooter? Mr Shooter, will you give me some mud off your boots? Mr Shooter, will you kiss my scarf?

"Stuff off!" Graeme Shooter railed and beckoned a steward over.

The steward pushed his way through the ranks of onlookers. "Are you really Graeme Shooter?" he said, looking puzzled.

"No, I'm the Wizard of Oz," said the striker. "I need to get to the players' entrance, preferably in the next two minutes."

"Why?" said the steward, raising his shoulders. He glanced into the back of the Venus Volcano and saw two boys wearing Denby Town scarves.

Q: WHO WAS THE FIRST BRITISH MANAGER TO WIN THE WORLD MANAGER OF THE YEAR AWARD?

"By the left," Graeme Shooter growled. "Is everyone in this place completely thick? I need to get on to the pitch, you berk."

The steward scratched his head. "Are you doing a presentation or something?"

"No, a flipping clog dance!" Graeme Shooter thundered, turning an irate shade of red. "I'm Graeme Shooter. I'm playing centre forward for Cranford United."

"Not on this pitch, you're not," said the steward.

"You what?" Graeme Shooter growled. "Is this a football ground or isn't it?"

The steward rubbed his chin. "Well, sort of," he said, looking embarrassed. "I'm afraid you're, well ... how can I put this? A little bit *out of position*, Mr Shooter. This *is* a football ground. A *rugby* football ground. You've come to the home of the Denby Bees."

"WHAT!" Graeme Shooter screeched. "But I can't have. I had directions from these two!"

The steward peered into the back of the car. "What two?" he asked.

Graeme Shooter whipped around.

The rear doors of the car were both wide open.

They were fluttering uncertainly in the breeze, not unlike the wings of a giant moth...

Quiz Answers

Magic!

p3   Alan Shearer. He hit five during 1995–96.

p4   Derby County.

p5   West Ham.

p6   Stockport County stuck thirteen goals passed the unfortunate keeper. It was Halifax's biggest ever defeat.

p7   Former Republic of Ireland manager Jack Charlton.

p8   Roger Milla (42) of Cameroon.

p9   Preston North End in 1888-89.

p10   The Wingless Wonders.

p11   Kevin Moran of Manchester United in 1985.

p12   Everton.

p14   Southampton.

p15   Emmanuel Petit of Arsenal hit France's winner in the 1998 final.

p16   Francis Lee hit thirteen for Manchester City in 1972.

p17   Kenny Dalglish.

The Lift

p21   In 1973, Maglioni of the Argentinian side, Independiente, thumped three past Gimnasia y Esgrima in just one minute and fifty seconds!

p22   West Bromwich Albion.

p23   Ray Wilkins.

p24   AC and Inter of Milan

p26   The Brazilian striker, Artur Friedenreich.

p27   Manchester United.

p28   Leslie Compton, aged thirty-eight.

p29   Wolverhampton Wanderers.

p30   Trevor Francis.

p31   Five.

p32   Norwich.

p33   Brian Clough.

p34   Dumbarton.

p35   Grimsby.

p36   Terry Venables (with Barcelona).

The New Kid

Redvers Brandling

Redvers Brandling's stories have appeared in many anthologies and have been adapted for children's radio and TV. His short story, *Jamie's Magic Christmas Present*, appeared in NICE ONE, SANTA!

Redvers is a lifelong Sunderland fan; still plays in the garden with his six grandsons and listens to jazz whilst recovering from injuries thus sustained.

"Wonder what he'll be like?"

As he spoke, Jason Hall, captain and midfielder for St Peter's football team, jabbed a thumb sideways. The thumb pointed at the new kid, Josh Stafford.

"He's big enough," replied Billy "Rocket" Watkins. Everybody called Billy "Rocket" and when you saw one of his shots you knew why!

"Yeah, but is he good enough?"

"Well, we'll soon find out."

It was a Tuesday afternoon games period, the sides were picked and shuffling into position.

"Right, let's get on with it," shouted Old Clarkie before his shrill whistle started the action. There was a brisk wind howling down the pitch and with this behind him, Jason took a back-pass from the kick-off and launched a high swirling punt towards the other team's goal.

"Get on to that one," he muttered as the ball began to drop.

"It's mine!"

The new kid's voice rang out commandingly. He was the biggest player on the field and his head of tight, curly hair seemed just about to nod clear when ... he changed his mind, ducked and...

Thunk.

Q: WHAT IS LIVERPOOL'S JACK BALMER FAMOUS FOR?

The ball landed on his back and dropped at the feet of the onrushing Rocket. In a crack it was in the back of the net for the first goal of the game.

The next hour passed quickly – as games periods always did. There'd been plenty of goals and excitement but Jason and Rocket were still on the same subject as they walked back to the changing rooms.

"What do you think now then?" asked Jason.

"Dunno really – for somebody who looks the part I've never seen so many ducks and dives and miskicks," replied Rocket.

"Yeah – seems useless... And yet..."

"I know what you're going to say. There's something not right. He looks as if he knows exactly what he's going to do – then suddenly does it all wrong."

"Weird," sighed Jason. "Maybe he's just nervous, being new and all that."

The next day in school was the usual routine stuff until just before dinner time. Then, for a few minutes, Old Clarkie was giving the class some quick fire questions on opposites. He gave the initial word, say "optimist", and there was a point for the first kid to shout "pessimist".

This, of course, was meat and drink to Ziggy Forbes, the class joker. While Julie, Jessica, Ralph and the other bright sparks fired back correct answers, he got the giggles going with the odd nonsense reply slipped in deliberately.

"Headmaster," snapped Mr Clarke.

Ziggy was in like a flash.

"Conkey Roberts."

Amidst the guffaws of laughter, Ziggy slapped a cupped hand

Q: WHICH SIDE'S FANS ARE KNOWN AS GOONERS?

over his mouth as if he'd made a genuine mistake. Mr Roberts, the headteacher, had a whopper of a nose – hence he was always referred to as "Conkey" (behind his back of course).

"Sir, sir. Headmistress." Jessica wasn't going to be put off getting the right answer, and a point.

But while all the hilarity was going on, Jason had been looking at Josh Stafford. The whole class had been laughing, even Clarkie was having a job keeping his face straight, but there was no smile on Josh's face. In fact, he was pretty much as he'd been ever since arriving – serious, tense and not much interested in anything – even football!

The next day there was no smile on Ziggy Forbes' face either. Along with several others in the class he was coughing and sneezing and blowing his nose every five minutes. By the time it was Friday, half the class were away with terrible colds.

"I don't know what we're going to do about tomorrow's match," said Mr Clarke to Jason at dinner time. Stroking his chin with his hand, the teacher was sitting with a piece of paper in front of him. On it was the shape of a football team – with too many empty spaces.

"We've never been so short of players as this," he went on.

"What about Josh, sir? He's big and he hasn't got a cold."

"You're right. If we play him and the two lads who were subs last week we can just about get a team together. But there's nobody left to be sub this week I'm afraid."

St Peter's was a small school but this season it had its best team for years. For the first time that anybody could remember they had a real chance of winning the District Under 12s league.

Q: HOW DID PICKLES SAVE THE WORLD CUP?

"It's a good job it's only Newborough we're playing," mused Jason. "We don't want to lose any points at this stage."

A little later, Jason and Rocket happened to be standing next to the noticeboard with the team on it when Josh came up. He was looking as serious as ever as he glanced casually at the board. When he read the contents his face went through two rapid changes. First, when he saw his own name, something like excitement lit up his face for a fleeting second. It was quickly replaced by an expression of sheer panic.

"I can't play," he gasped. "I just can't."

"Oh don't worry," said Jason, punching the new boy encouragingly on the arm. "Newborough aren't that good anyway."

"We usually duff 'em up easy," chirped Rocket.

"It's not that ... no ... I just can't," muttered Josh.

"But look," went on Jason. "We've only got eleven fit men. Old Clarkie's going to go mad if you don't play."

"But ... but ... if my mum..." Without finishing, Josh suddenly turned and hurried away.

Just after home time that afternoon, Jason and Rocket saw him in deep conversation with Mr Clarke. They were just near enough to hear the teacher's closing remark.

"No, no. We won't worry her about it ... there'll be no problem."

Saturday morning arrived cold and blustery with threatening clouds squeezing out regular flurries of snowflakes. St Peter's were in their usual red and white stripes. Defender Josh Stafford was kitted out entirely in borrowed gear – the "problem"

Q: CAN YOU NAME THE TWO ENGLISH LEAGUE SIDES WHO PLAY THEIR HOME MATCHES AT A ST JAMES PARK?

Mr Clarke had sorted out for him. Bottom of the league New-borough kicked in nervously in their dark blue shirts and shorts.

As soon as the match started it was obvious why Newborough were having such a bad season. Poor passes and bad marking allowed St Peter's to sweep forward time and again.

"This time!"

Midfielder Elroy Butcher shouted impatiently as he slid the umpteenth through ball to Rocket. But Rocket still had the coughs and sneezes and was right off form. His quickly taken shot whistled well wide.

"Never mind, Rock," consoled Jason, putting an arm round the shoulder of the disconsolate striker. "With this wind behind us we'll get three before half-time."

But they didn't, and you could sense the relief in the New-borough side as they lined up with the wind behind them in the second half. Up to now the St Peter's defence had had nothing to do, but with increasing confidence Newborough began to thump long high balls towards them.

"They won't beat us this way," thought Jason as he trapped another aimless punt and eased it forward for Elroy.

"Wayne," yelled the midfielder as he hit a crossfield pass to the left wing. Once again however the wind caught the ball and held it up.

"Come for it, Josh," shouted winger, Wayne Crum, as the pass faded behind him.

He needn't have shouted, for Josh Stafford had anticipated what was going to happen. Perfectly positioned and seemingly in complete control, he then lunged wildly at the ball which spun

Q: WHO IS HOLLAND'S ALL-TIME LEADING
GOALSCORER?

past his right foot and bounced on to the knee of the onrushing striker. Only the quick reaction of goalie Ollie Simpson saved the situation as he raced out of his penalty area and belted the ball into touch.

"Come on you lot. Wake up and mark these men!" he complained.

"Long throw – quick!" urged the Newborough captain.

It came as directed and within seconds the ball was bobbing like a mad thing from head to foot in the St Peter's penalty area. There were cries of panic.

"Clear it!"

"Get it out!"

"Mark up!"

Then the ball was at the feet of the Newborough striker. As he drew his foot back to shoot, the large figure of Josh crashed into him in a hopelessly mistimed tackle.

Penalty!

The grounded forward got up with a grin. Spotting the ball he took a short run and cracked it past Ollie Simpson.

St Peter's nil, Newborough one – and the visitors were now confident it was going to be their day.

"Come on, come on, we can still do it," urged Jason, as St Peter's kicked off, but within minutes Newborough were again surging into the attack. This time they won a corner on the left. Their penalty-taker ran over to cross it and fired in a fast-moving, head-high ball.

"Mine!" yelled Ollie, racing out of his goal.

But he was wrong. Just as he was at full stretch, Josh leapt in front of him and got his head to the ball. In a flash it skidded past

Q: WHO WERE THE FIRST NON-BRITISH SIDE TO AVOID DEFEAT AGAINST ENGLAND IN AN INTERNATIONAL FIXTURE?

the goalkeeper's desperate lunge and cracked into the top corner of the net. Own goal.

There was a horrible silence in the St Peter's defence – and then the referee's whistle sounded for full time.

St Peter's nil, Newborough two.

A dejected Jason was peeling off his boots a few minutes later when he was aware of somebody standing over him.

"I'm really sorry about that."

It was Josh, looking about as miserable as it was possible to be.

Jason had heard some of the snide comments which had been directed at the new boy after the final whistle and, despite everything, he felt sorry for him.

"Just an off day," he said tersely. "You'll be better next time."

"There won't be a next time," replied Josh firmly and quietly. "I'm never going to play again."

As Jason looked up, the new boy turned away with a sigh, muttering "Perhaps she was right after all."

By Sunday afternoon, Jason had forgotten about the disappointment of the match and his chat with Josh. He and his sister Julie were watching TV when Mum called to them.

"Hey you two, I want you to take some clean washing over to Gran's."

"Oh no – do we have to?" groaned Julie.

"Yes, you have to," Mum replied. "You can go on your bikes and put the stuff in your saddle-bags."

"OK," muttered the reluctant pair.

A few minutes later they were off – and on to one of their favourite topics of conversation.

 **Q:** WHICH TOP-FLIGHT ENGLISH CLUB WAS THE FIRST TO EXPERIMENT WITH UNDERSOIL HEATING?

"Man U are certs for the league now," said Julie, who was a walking encyclopedia as far as football was concerned.

"I reckon Arsenal or Liverpool could still catch them, even Chelsea."

"Not a chance. Here – let's go through the estate. It'll save some time."

The sprawling Dean Court Estate was a mixture. Some posh old Victorian houses stood on the edge of it, then modern semis, then flats and long blocks of garages. They were pedalling past one of the latter when they saw a lone figure kicking a ball against the far wall of the garage block.

"Got another David Beckham there, look," nodded Julie.

"Hang on, let's watch him for a bit – but keep back so he doesn't see us," replied Jason.

In the distance the lone footballer was unaware of their presence. With alternate feet he crashed the ball angrily against the brick wall, either trapping the rebounds stone dead or volleying them accurately back towards the same spot. Then he began flicking the rebounds in the air, heading the ball gently and then dropping it to hit on the half-volley.

It was a very impressive display of skill and a tight-lipped Jason wondered why Josh Stafford couldn't produce it for the benefit of St Peter's football team.

The next morning Jason grabbed Rocket the minute he came through the school gates.

"You should have seen him. It was all there – trapping, kicking, shooting, heading – none of those miskicks and lunges he does in matches. I tell you he's a natural."

Q: WHICH ENGLISH SIDE COUNTS NOEL AND LIAM GALLAGHER AMONGST ITS FANS?

"But who. . .?" began Rocket, who was surprised at the anger in Jason's voice.

"The Stafford kid of course," rasped Jason impatiently, "I tell you I saw him and—"

"Then why has he been playing like a no-hoper for us?" queried the ace striker.

"I don't know, but I mean to find out. Watch it – here he comes."

Through the school entrance came the tall figure of Josh, looking miserable as usual.

"Wotcha Josh," called Rocket, as he and Jason strolled over to meet the newcomer.

"Oh. . . Er. . . Hi."

"Been playing any football over the weekend?" asked Jason pointedly.

"Er. . . No. . . I don't like football. You know that."

"I know one thing – you're a liar."

"What do you mean? You've no right—"

"I saw you on Sunday afternoon – and I've got a witness."

"You. . . You saw me what?"

"Kicking a football against some garages, and you were loving it, and you were great. Now how about telling us why you don't play like that for the school team. Well, what about it?"

As he listened to Jason's angry voice, Josh's face went through one of its rapid changing routines. First he blushed brilliant red then, with a look of determined stubbornness, he turned quickly and began to hurry away.

"Hey, hang on," snapped Rocket, reaching out to grab the other boy's PE bag.

 **Q:** WHICH WELSH INTERNATIONAL RECEIVED THE QUICKEST EVER YELLOW CARD DURING AN FA CUP MATCH?

Josh tried to wrench it away, and as he did so the bag pulled open and fell to the ground. There, stencilled on the inside of the cover, was a name: Joshua Lawrence.

"Here – what's this?" queried Jason. "This isn't yours."

"It is!" hissed Josh, seizing the bag and bundling it tightly under his arm. "It is – now leave me alone!"

Jason was never one for telling tales but when Old Clarkie sent for him at playtime, to discuss the team for the next match, the whole mysterious story of Josh – his hidden skill and the strange name on the bag – all slipped out.

"What did you say the name was?" asked Mr Clarke again.

"Lawrence, sir. Joshua Lawrence."

"Lawrence," mused Mr Clarke, "Lawrence... I wonder if it could be possible? All right Jason, we'll play our friend Josh again on Wednesday night."

"But do you think he'll play as he really can do sir ... or..."

"We'll just have to wait and see."

But even as he spoke, the teacher had a faraway look in his eye. "I wonder..."

When the teams ran on to the pitch on Wednesday night, there was a good sprinkling of spectators round the ground. Conditions were perfect for football, and Lowfield, top of the league and unbeaten all season, looked ready to make the most of them. They attacked from the kick-off.

After five minutes the Lowfield right winger took a long pass out of defence and raced forward. Skipping over an Elroy Butcher tackle he reached the byline and fired over a low skimming cross. As usual Josh was in the right position,

Q: WHICH ENGLISH SIDE WERE THE INSPIRATION FOR EUROPEAN SUPER-CLUB JUVENTUS' KIT?

performing the wrong action. A wild lunge caused the ball to spin off his left foot and, fortunately, fizz straight back to a surprised Ollie Simpson.

The quick thinking goalie, realizing he couldn't pick up what might be considered a back-pass, tried to dribble the ball forward before kicking upfield. In a flash the Lowfield striker was on to him. Both players went down in a heap and the ball spun back to the right winger.

"GOAL!"

The Lowfield fans were already celebrating as the angled shot sped towards the net. But they were too soon. With a super-human effort Jason got back and, with a diving header, diverted the ball round the post for a corner.

"Fantastic Jase," gasped Ollie, scrambling to his feet. "But you," he snarled, glowering at Josh, "You're useless – shouldn't be in the team at all."

"Yeah well... I don't want to be anyway," snapped the miserable looking Josh.

"Shut up the pair of you," called Jason. "Now come on – concentrate!"

The corner was cleared but this action was just the start of a half of intense Lowfield pressure and they soon had a two-goal cushion. St Peter's fought hard but two–nil to Lowfield at half-time was fair to both sides.

"Don't worry lads, you're doing all right. You can turn it round this half."

Mr Clarke was his usual encouraging self at the break, but he did look a bit uncertain and kept glancing towards the school gates.

Q: WHO ARE THE SILK MEN?

The second half started like the first, with fierce pressure from Lowfield. Within seconds they got a corner on the right. As the players jostled each other in the penalty area, Old Clarkie's voice shouted in support.

"Come on St Peter's. Mark your men."

Then a second, female voice, backed his up.

"Come on St Peter's. You can do it."

The effect of the second voice on Josh Stafford was electric. Glancing towards the touchline, a look of sheer joy crossed his face as he saw the tall, fair-haired lady standing next to Mr Clarke.

"Watch it!"

Jason's command brought everybody back to concentrating on the corner. This time, as the ball came ranging across Josh was not only in the right position but he rose to head away powerfully. Lowfield, perhaps over-confident, were caught unprepared by the length of the header – but Rocket wasn't.

Dragging the ball forward with the outside of his left foot he set off straight down the middle of the pitch towards the Lowfield goal.

"Get back!"

"Cover him..."

"Goalie!"

There were shouts of confusion from the surprised defenders. They might as well have saved their breath. Fifteen yards out Rocket cracked a left-foot shot that tore high into the top corner of the net.

Lowfield two, St Peter's one.

Q: WHICH FRENCH STAR WON THE COVETED EUROPEAN FOOTBALLER OF THE YEAR AWARD FOR AN AMAZING THREE CONSECUTIVE SEASONS IN THE EIGHTIES?

"What's got into him?" asked Rocket, nodding towards a grinning Josh as he and Jason ran back to the centre-circle.

"Dunno – but let's make the most of it. Come on!" replied Jason.

The key feature of the rest of the game was the complete transformation of Josh Stafford. Now he was like a man inspired. One minute he was clearing up a Lowfield attack, the next he was surging upfield in support of his forwards.

Lowfield were still playing terrific football but justice was done just two minutes from the final whistle. Jason trapped a loose ball in midfield and slid it through to Rocket. The sharpshooter was off at his usual gallop with tired defenders streaming in his wake. Level with the penalty area he hit a fast, rising shot that seemed a certain goal – until the goalie, leaping to his left, made a brilliant save by flicking the ball on to the bar.

With a resounding thud the ball rebounded over the head of Rocket and the chasing Lowfield defenders. There, following up, was Josh. Calmly he trapped the ball with his right foot, glanced up, then lobbed it with his left foot over the still stranded goalkeeper. The ball arched gracefully and triumphantly into the net.

"Goal... Goal... GOAL!"

The St Peter's fans roared their delight just as the final whistle blew. A great match had ended in a fair result.

"I reckon you must have something to tell us," said Jason to Josh as the end of match cheers died down and Mr Clarke stopped shaking the fair-haired lady's hand.

"You're right. I owe the whole team an explanation," agreed Josh as Rocket joined them.

Q: WHERE DO TOTTENHAM HOTSPUR PLAY THEIR HOME GAMES?

Later, when everybody had changed, they all crowded round Josh.

"The only thing I've ever been any good at was football," he began.

"Huh – you could have fooled us," snorted Ollie Simpson.

"Yeah, well, you see, my name used to be Josh Lawrence and my dad—"

"You mean you're Skippy Lawrence's son?" gasped Rocket.

There was an embarrassed silence. Skippy Lawrence – a player who'd spent most of his career in the lower divisions – had become a hero of them all when he'd joined Millchaster Rovers two years ago and broken all scoring records. Picked for England last season, he'd been injured in the match and, when travelling home by car, had been involved in a crash...

"When my dad was killed in the car crash," went on Josh quietly, "my mum blamed his injury – and football – for causing it. So, the last thing she wanted was for me to have anything at all to do with the game any more. She even changed our name to Stafford so nobody could make any connection when we moved here and—"

"And," came a calm voice in the doorway, "it took your Mr Clarke to make me see sense again."

There stood the tall, fair-haired lady with a smiling Mr Clarke beside her.

"Good Old Clarkie!" shouted Rocket (from behind his hand of course).

Somehow, everybody felt better with the laughter which followed.

Fantasy Football

Chris Wooding

Chris Wooding is twenty-two and lives in Leicester. He writes books and stories because he doesn't want to get a real job. He thinks his attitude is shocking and urges nobody to follow his example.

Chris's first soccer story, *Back Seat Manager*, appeared in NICE ONE, SANTA! His excellent fantasy series, BROKEN SKY, is also available from Scholastic.

I t was one of those really *big* dragons. You know, the old-school kind. All scaly and 'orrible and with a foul temper. *You'd* have a temper like that if you had a three-thousand-year cramp from sitting on a pile of gold and magic swords and all that stuff. That was why us humans always beat dragons in the end. We usually got a good night's sleep before the fight.

Anyway, there was me and Boric the Barbarian and Fey the elf, all hidden down in the bushes on a hillside, watching the Evil team's dragon come soaring towards us. Our own dragon had been daft enough to take on the Black Paladin earlier in the game, ignoring hundreds of years of legends in which the knight invariably slays the big overgrown lizard. There's always one.

So we're stuck trying to intercept *this* guy, because he's got the sphere and if he gets past us, there's nothing to stop him flying right into our goal and winning the game. Most of our aerial defence got taken out by the Evil Wizard, who came up with a storm that caught our flyers out in the open. Our Hawkmen got their feathers blown off. Our Griffin flew into a mountain in the poor visibility. Our Pegasus got cooked by a bolt of lightning – Boric was absently chewing on one of its legs that he had thoughtfully removed and brought along.

"We're gonna lose this year if we don't bring that thing down," I commented.

"Fear not," said Boric. "The forces of Evil shall not take this day."

Q: WHO IS THE ONLY PLAYER TO HAVE SCORED A HAT-TRICK IN A WORLD CUP FINAL?

Boric always says stuff like that. But he's a hero, so he can get away with it. Basically, it was looking pretty bad for the Good team right now. And all we had to take out this dragon with was an elf and his golden bow.

I don't like elves. Nobody likes elves. They're only on the side of Good because they're too sappy to do anything nasty. If we were picking teams, they'd be the ones who were always left till last. They mince around uselessly singing songs and playing on their lutes, and whenever they get tackled they go down and roll around wailing and holding their shins. However, one thing they *are* good at is nailing things with arrows.

And so we waited, while he nocked and aimed and rolled his shoulders and made a big show of it all.

"May your arrow fly true, friend elf," Boric intoned.

"Just shoot it, will ya?" I added, fingering the lucky nutmeg that hung on a cord around my neck. Don't ask me why, I've just always carried one. Stops me getting travel sick.

Fey let go. We watched, holding our breath, as the arrow streaked towards its target ... and let out a cheer as the dragon roared and dropped the sphere. Our cheer faded as it turned its baleful eyes on us. Fey had only shot it in the foot.

"Why didn't you kill it?" I cried.

"Even a dragon has the right to live," Fey said sniffily.

"He's a bad guy! He's on the Evil side!"

"Who says he's evil? What's he done?"

"This is football," I grated. "The opponent's side is *always* Evil."

Any further arguments would have to wait. I wasn't sticking around for that angry dragon to come get us, and besides,

Q: CAN YOU NAME THE TWO ENGLISH PLAYERS WHO HAVE REACHED THE EUROPEAN CUP FINAL WITH TWO DIFFERENT CLUBS?

somewhere down in those woods was the sphere. Those horrible, dark, goblin-infested woods.

Football. It's a beautiful game.

I suppose I should explain a bit, bring you up to speed. It's Festmastide today, the day when the whole land celebrates something called Christmas. Christmas hasn't actually happened yet, but that doesn't stop us celebrating it. It's all to do with the Mad Prophet Tolkien, who made some pretty nifty predictions before falling foul of those nasty Barrow-wights a few years ago. One of them was this Christmas thing, which I guess you all know about. The other was about football.

See, he reckoned that sometime in the far, far future there would be a game, invented in a place called Ingerland. It would involve two neighbouring villages, and an inflated pig's bladder. So far, so good. The object of the game would be to kick, throw or carry the bladder to your opponent's village; whoever did this first was the winner. They were pretty much the rules. And, for some reason, they called this football.

Over the years, it changed a lot more, and people actually *had* to kick the ball, and you couldn't just punch out your opponent if he got in your way. They brought in things called referees, who everyone hated coz they stopped players doing what they most wanted to: beating each other senseless. But that first game was the start of what was to become the world's most popular sport.

Well, we never miss the chance of a celebration. So when the Mad Prophet popped his clogs, we decided to combine the two prophecies into Festmastide. No one much liked the idea of a pig's bladder, so we used a shiny metal sphere instead. And

Q: WHO HOLDS THE RECORD FOR THE MOST GOALS SCORED IN THE FA CUP?

villages had a habit of being burned to the ground by dragons, so wizard's towers were a safer bet for the goals. Other than that, it was pretty much the same.

My name's Skank, and I'll be your commentator for the evening. I'm also a thief. That's a job description, not a confession. Thieving is big business round here. Not just anyone can be a thief, y'know. You have to pass the Guild exams and get an Equity card and everything.

Now I'm a kinda small and scrawny kid, but with me is Boric. He's one of those apprentice barbarian hero types – he's got posters of Conan on his wall back home. He's only a couple of years older than me, but he's got muscles on his muscles and that, coupled with a diabolically out-of-date haircut, gets him all the girls. We're sort of a double act. Well, what I mean is, he gets to do all the hero stuff and I get to be his sidekick. Guys like me don't win games for a team. We just make up the numbers.

"Accursed goblin! Hold still while I cleft thee in twain!"

The goblins were, predictably, all over the sphere by the time we got to it. We had bravely sent Fey off as a decoy for the dragon while we went down to the woods. It was only fair. He was the one who wanted to let it live.

Boric was having a fine old time swinging his axe around. He was keeping the goblins at bay while I went to pick up the sphere. They had been occupied with worshipping it or something, rather than taking it back to their team like they should have done. Goblins are stupid.

Once the shiny black sphere was cradled in my arms, we beat a

 **Q:** ALONG WITH GEOFF HURST, WHICH OTHER ENGLISH PLAYER HAS SCORED A RECORD FORTY-SIX LEAGUE CUP GOALS?

quick retreat into the woods. The pursuit tailed off after a while, and we dropped our pace a little.

"You love all this hack-and-slay stuff, don't you?" I said to my friend.

"There was never an opponent whom I could not defeat with mine mighty strength," Boric replied, firming his considerable chin. "And I have won the Festmastide game of football for the side of Good three years running."

As if I needed reminding. "Aren't you worried, though?" I said. "What if this year they put someone stronger than you in goal?"

"Football is a game of strength," Boric replied. "The strongest and fastest survive. I shall beat all who face me."

I scratched the back of my neck and sighed. Boric was an OK guy, but when it came to football . . . ugh. Funny how the game turned normal people into mouthy, arrogant ball-hogs as soon as they thought they were good.

He was right, though. The strongest and fastest survived. And that meant I was never going to be one of football's heroes. Not that I really *wanted* to be, but . . . well, it would be nice to steal some of Boric's thunder for a change. Score one for the small guys.

I was still carrying the sphere when I got tackled.

I don't know how they sneaked up on us. We were just coming to the edge of the forest when they struck. I was thinking how we were going to get into the Evil tower, wondering who they would have in goal, and what kind of defence they had. I suppose that was why I wasn't listening out.

Q: WHERE WOULD YOU FIND THE TOON ARMY?

Well, they got us anyway. Four ugly, smelly orcs. The first I knew of it was when my breath was knocked out of me and I went sprawling. The next thing, the sphere was being wrenched out from beneath my body. By then I'd realized what was going on, and I was hanging on to it for dear life, but the orcs were tougher than me. They tore it out of my hands.

"Begone, evil scum!" Boric yelled, picking a line at random from the Clichéd Battle Cry Manual before rushing in to attack. By then I'd already booted one of the orcs in the unmentionables. Later on, they'd give things called red cards for that, according to the Mad Prophet. But in these liberated times, we could do what we liked.

Boric went slicing left and right with his axe, getting the orcs off me. I didn't need any help, mind you, but it made him feel better to try. The one with the sphere was making a break for it, and Boric went roaring off after him into the trees, leaving the rest of the orcs to limp and stagger away.

I was nursing my bruised ribs when Boric came back, carrying the sphere and wearing a triumphant grin.

"So, friend Skank, you see that a swift pair of legs and strong body beats any opponent in this game," he crowed.

"One day you're gonna come up against something you can't out-muscle," I griped. "*Then* what are you gonna do? Football's about *thinking*; strength and speed are only half of it. It's skill and brains that matter."

"Ho! Art thou jealous, little thief? May I remind you that—"

"*You have won the Festmastide game of football for the side of Good three years running*," I mimicked, bobbing my head from side to side as I spoke. "I know. Chuck me the sphere."

Q: WHICH GERMAN MIDFIELDER HAS PARTICIPATED IN MORE WORLD CUP FINALS MATCHES THAN ANY OTHER PLAYER?

Boric hesitated. "I think not," he said. "Perhaps it is safer in my hands. For the good of the team."

"Yeah," I said. "Right."

The Evil tower stood on a hill just beyond the forest. It was a tall, narrow thing, with crenellations at the top like you get on castle walls. A single, high archway was set into its base. That was the goal. Get the sphere in there – whether it was punched, carried, or still wrapped in the skin of the opponent you kicked it through – and you won the game.

Lots of fringe benefits came with being the goalscorer on Festmastide; not least a lucrative line in sponsorships and your name in the history books. Huh! Like *that* was gonna happen. Guys like Boric make history; people like me just get to watch it go by. If I'd have been blessed with his strength and stamina (without being cursed with his brain) then *I* could've been remembered for something. Who remembers a thief? Oh, except for that Robin Hood guy from Knot-in-Ham the Mad Prophet harped on about, but he's not even a twinkle in the woodsman's eye yet.

Oops! Sidetracking. Sorry. Anyway, the Evil tower. Naturally, it was dark and brooded with menace, and ravens croaked around its heights yadda yadda yah etc. You know what an Evil tower looks like, right? It's all an intimidation tactic. Old hands like me and Boric knew that it was all special effects. The ravens were from Crows'R'Us and forced to chain-smoke all day to achieve the correct hoarseness in their caw. And yes, ravens *are* crows, except one wing is shorter than the other, which is why their only purpose in life is to

Q: WHICH SIDE'S HOME MATCHES ARE PLAYED AT THE CITY GROUND?

find something nice and sinister to circle around. Otherwise their crow mates would laugh at them for not being able to fly in a straight line.

We watched the tower from the shelter of the trees. The defence was pretty heavy. Presumably the dragon had fried Fey by now and reported how we'd stolen the sphere and were on our way. Six orcs waited around the goalmouth, with the biggest, most vicious-looking ogre in goal. And standing on the flat roof of the tower was Malebog, the enemy wizard, all done out in black and red robes and wearing a great, horned helmet. His aura of Wizardly Power™ was slightly rumpled because he had to keep swatting away the ravens that perched on the tip of the longest horn, but we knew what he was capable of.

We had reinforcements, too. Dwarf the dwarf, who was so fiercely proud of his dwarfishness that he had changed his name so no one would forget it. And O'Leary the leprechaun, from a place in the future called Oyerlund, who'd got lost rainbow-surfing on the way to his pot of gold and ended up here. We really *had* to have him along, if only because he was such a bad ambassador for his country, fulfilling every cliché that history could come up with. Besides, everyone loves foreign players, and the team had a healthy line of shamrocks and Blarney stones in the local gift shop.

It was time to attack.

"OK, here's the deal," I said, hunkering down with them all. "Now, we know Malebog is gonna be stopping O'Leary using his teleporting power to get into the eighteen-yard box—"

"Begorrah, and 'tis a shameful thing, so 'tis, so 'tis," he murmured.

Q: WHO WERE THE LAST SIDE TO WIN THE OLD FIRST DIVISION TITLE BEFORE IT BECAME THE PREMIERSHIP?

"But he'll still be able to flit around outside that," I continued. "So if he gets in the clear, pass and we'll—"

"Nay!" bellowed Boric, and everyone frantically shushed him, sweating as we did so and casting nervous glances at the enemy team nearby. "Nay," he said again, quieter. "I shall carry the sphere to victory, using mine own great strength to defeat the ogre. You mortals ... err ... team-mates keep the wizard from working his vile magic upon me."

"Don't be dumb, Boric, that ogre will turn you inside out and floss with your intestines," I said.

"Who hath the sphere?" he demanded. It was a rhetorical question. " 'Tis I!" he roared, and leaped from cover to go racing towards the tower. "With me, men!" he called, holding his axe high with one hand, the sphere clutched to his chest in the other.

"He's a reckless young feller, so he is," said O'Leary.

"Needs some time in the mines, is what he needs," grumbled Dwarf. "Teach him some patience."

I sighed. "Are we going or what?"

We burst out of the undergrowth and charged after our fearless hero, Boric. Fearless and stupid, of course.

Well, it all went off then. Three of the orcs took one look at us and charged. That's the best thing about orcs; they're too disorganized to make an effective defence. Three of them stayed behind with the ogre. And Malebog was cooking up some kind of spell or other.

"Orcs! I hate orcs!" Dwarf raged, pounding after Boric to get tied up in the brawl. I was sticking close to him. The best way to avoid getting turned into something horrible by Malebog was to hang near a dwarf. Nothing had better magic resistance than a

Q: WHICH SIDE HOLDS THE RECORD FOR THE BIGGEST MARGIN OF VICTORY IN AN ENGLISH PREMIER LEAGUE MATCH?

dwarf; they were so infuriatingly practical that they simply refused to believe in it. For some reason, this worked wonders, and while his team-mates were being toasted or transformed into Welsh dressers, you could bet a dwarf would be happily ambling along, immune to the bolts of multicoloured death that flew all around him.

Well, the other thing about dwarves is that they hate orcs. Nobody knows why. Not even dwarves. It's just written in some rule book somewhere.

Boric and Dwarf laid into the orcs that had run out to get us. It wasn't much of a challenge.

"O'Leary!" I shouted. "Get up there and stop that wizard!"

"Sure, and I'll be your footstool an' all, y'filthy rogue," he grumbled, before puffing on his corncob pipe and disappearing in a shower of Lucky Charms.

I put my hand on the nutmeg that hung round my neck, sending a silent prayer to Filch, God of Thieves, to keep me safe. Then I ploughed on in.

The three orcs had been despatched with ease. Boric and Dwarf were piling off towards the goal. I ran left, waiting for a pass in case they got into trouble. Yeah, *sure*. Boric would rather die than pass to me at a crucial moment like this. Not *strong* or *fast* enough.

Looking at that ogre, I wasn't sure if he'd have a choice in the matter anyway.

I glanced up at the tower in time to see O'Leary disappearing under a shrieking, flapping mass of black feathers as the ravens set to work on him. Hmm, guess they *do* have more than ornamental value. Unfortunately, that meant Malebog was still free

Q: WHICH SPANISH SIDE HAVE WON MORE EUROPEAN TROPHIES THAN ANY OTHER TEAM?

to cast his spell; and he was brewing up a rooster by the looks of things.

Boric ducked the orcs' swords and shoved them aside, pushing through as if they were nothing, heading for the ogre who stood square in the goal. Dwarf had other ideas, going for the orcs instead. He was in the mind for a ruck, apparently.

While the orcs were busy with Dwarf, I nipped round them to run shotgun with Boric.

"Kiss my axe, thou chewer of dung!" Boric yelled, swinging his weapon one-handed at the enormous, fanged, musclebound ogre that stood in his way.

The ogre caught his wrist and twisted. The axe fell free.

"Er…" said Boric, and then the ogre's fist prevented any other sounds coming out of his mouth.

I winced as the ogre set to pounding on my heroic buddy, bouncing him off various hard surfaces before punting him back over the treeline. But, well, sympathy only stretched so far. It was his own dumb fault. I, in the meantime, was occupied with unobtrusively stealing the sphere from where it had fallen out of Boric's hands.

Now I'm a *good* thief. If it had been just me and the ogre, I'd have taxed it without him even seeing me. But it was Malebog's roar that gave me away. That, and the blue fireball he sent streaking down after me. One look at that and I knew the game was up; it was a homing fireball, and it had its sights on yours truly.

The ogre leaped back in front of the goal, blocking my way. I had only a moment to act.

You don't have brawn, you're not fast, I thought. *So use your brain!*

Q: WHICH SIDE HOLDS THE ENGLISH RECORD FOR THE MOST WINS AT THE START OF A LEAGUE SEASON?

I'm a pretty quick thinker, I'll give myself that. And seeing the ogre standing there, crouched low, legs astride to spread his weight, I had an idea. Reaching into my shirt, I pulled out my lucky nutmeg pendant and tore it free. Then I threw it at the goalie.

Sound stupid? Well, it was, I guess. Worked, though.

I'm a pretty good shot with stones and things. Nutmegs weren't much different. So I was running at him as I threw, and the thing hit him square between the eyes with a pathetic *doink* noise. Behind me, I could hear the crackling fireball racing closer.

I dropped the sphere and kicked it. Right at the ogre, along the ground.

He was too surprised by what had hit him in the face to prevent what was happening; and as the sphere rolled through his legs, and I slipped behind him like an eel, all he could do was make a puzzled "Uh?" sound.

The fireball was still on track for me. However, now I was behind the ogre, he was kinda in the way. Unfortunate, that.

I booted the sphere at the open goalmouth (breaking all my toes . . . it *was* metal) at the exact moment that the ogre valiantly took the brunt of Malebog's fireball. The sphere soared underneath the arch, into the Evil tower, and a great cheer went up from the side of Good. Well, those who had survived, anyway.

For a moment, I couldn't believe it. I had *scored*? I had *won* it?

"Great move, my boy," said Dwarf, slapping me on the lower back as I limped away from the charred slab of ogre that had been their goalie. "What do you call it?"

Q: WHO WERE THE FIRST SIDE TO BE AUTOMATICALLY RELEGATED FROM THE FOOTBALL LEAGUE?

"Uuuh..." I said. "The Nutmeg?"

Dwarf laughed. "You call that a name? What about ... the Ogre Destroyer? Or the Death Shimmy? History will record this moment, boy! Who's going to remember the *Nutmeg*?'

"I don't know," I said, smiling. "I just have this feeling..."

Mike's Lucky Sock

Iain Stansfield

For K

Iain Stansfield was born in Manchester in 1968. He is a full-time lawyer and part-time children's story writer. His short story, *My Mascot Misery*, appeared in NICE ONE, SANTA!

Although he now lives in London, Iain is a staunch Manchester City season-ticket holder. He is also very proud of the fact that he once met Dennis Tueart.

The Market Street Marauders trudged off the pitch and into the changing room. They had lost six-nil. It was their seventh defeat on the run and left them anchored to the bottom of the District League.

Mike, the Marauders' centre forward, was taking it particularly hard: his shots on goal had hit the goalkeeper, the post, the crossbar, the corner flag and, on one occasion, the linesman. Everywhere but the back of the net.

He sat with his head in his hands as Mr Harris, the Marauders' manager, tried to lift the team.

"Come on, lads. Heads up. We can turn this around. It's just a question of not playing so badly."

The lads groaned. Mr Harris was not a great motivator.

"No, it's true. We just need to score some goals," Mr Harris continued, showing that he did at least understand the rules.

Mike looked up and addressed his team-mates. "Look, you lot, I'm sorry about all that out there. I should have buried those chances."

Mike's mate, Paul, spoke up. "Forget it, Mike. We were all rubbish. It's not just you."

The lads nodded. None of them had played well.

"OK, everyone," said Mr H, seeing there was no point in dwelling on today's performance. "Next Saturday we've got Deepdale. The week after it's the first round of the District Cup. Still plenty to play for. See you next week."

Q: WHICH TWO ITALIAN SERIE A TEAMS PLAY THEIR HOME FIXTURES AT THE STADIO OLIMPICO?

* * *

"How did you get on, Mike?" asked his dad when he got home.

"Six-nil," grunted Mike.

There was no need to ask who'd won. Mike ate his dinner in silence, or as near to silence as possible with his mum and dad yakking on, then skulked upstairs.

Mike slumped on his bed and opened his "Super Striker" annual. He'd got the book for Christmas. It had been one of his better presents and he'd read almost all of it. It had certainly been better than that pair of musical novelty reindeer socks his mum had given him. Mike shuddered at the memory.

On page sixty-eight he found an article called "Matchday Superstitions". It was about the weird things top footballers do to bring them luck. Apparently, some players always put their kit on in a certain order. Some Rangers defender Mike hadn't heard of, and who looked a bit fat, always ate pizza for breakfast on matchdays.

There were better ones, though. One of the strikers for the French World Cup winning team always spat three times on the halfway line before kick-off. The Marauders could do with some of that luck. If France could win the World Cup, the Market Street Marauders should be able to win a few District League matches and the odd cup-tie.

From now on Mike would have his own matchday superstition. It couldn't hurt.

The following Saturday was matchday. Mike tried to get his mum to give him pizza for breakfast. She told him that was

Q: WHICH STATS OBSESSED COMMENTATOR ONCE SAID: "AND STUART PEARCE HAS GOT THE TASTE OF WEMBLEY IN HIS NOSTRILS."?

disgusting and that toast was all he was getting. So much for *that* matchday superstition. He would have to try something else.

Mike went and called for Paul. They walked to the ground together.

"Paul, when you're getting changed for the match, what order do you put your stuff on?" asked Mike.

"You what?"

"Do you put your shorts on before your shirt? Do your socks go on last? That kind of thing."

"Nah. My socks don't go on last. They'd look daft on the outside of my boots."

Walking on, Mike figured out that he always put his shorts on first, then his shirt, then his socks and boots. This was the sequence which had doomed the Marauders to seven straight defeats. It would not be repeated.

As Mr Harris read the team out and gave his usual inspiring team-talk ("Lads, let's try not to be rubbish this week, eh?"), Mike concentrated. First he put on his socks and boots. Then he tried to drag his shorts on over them. Unfortunately, they were too tight and they got caught in the studs. Mike fell forwards off the bench trying to untangle them.

"Mike! Pay attention, lad. What are you playing at? Do we need to get your mum in here to dress you?" The team roared with laughter.

"Sorry. They're on now," Mike said, hoping all this would be worth it. He put his shirt on and trotted out for the warm-up.

As the match got ready to kick off, Mike and Paul stood over the ball at the centre circle. The ref was counting the players and setting his watch. As he was doing this, Mike bent over and spat

Q: CAN YOU NAME THE TWO DUTCH STARS TO HAVE WON THREE EUROPEAN FOOTBALLER OF THE YEAR AWARDS DURING THEIR CAREERS?

very slowly and deliberately on the ground, trying to hit the halfway line. True to his recent form in front of goal, he missed.

The ref was lifting his whistle to his mouth when he noticed Mike.

"What's wrong, lad?" he shouted. "Are you sick? Someone get this lad off the field!"

Mike tried to reassure the ref, but his mouth was full. He spat again, determined to hit the line. Mr Harris came running on with his sponge (he never ran on to the field without it) and led Mike off.

"Mike, are you OK?"

"I'm fine. Really."

"It looked like you were going to be sick."

Mike couldn't tell Mr Harris what he was trying to do because he was sure it would sound daft. Particularly after the shorts entanglement episode in the changing room.

"I can't let you play, Mike. Sorry. League regulations. I can't risk it. Ian! You're on. Centre forward."

Mike put on a tracksuit and watched the Marauders slump to a five-nil defeat. They were never in the game.

Great, thought Mike. I look a berk, get substituted and then we get hammered.

The matchday superstitions were not going well.

At home that evening, after reassuring his mum that he was fine (Mr Harris had telephoned), Mike got out "Super Striker" again and turned to page sixty-eight.

Among the matchday superstitions was one he hadn't noticed before. Darren Something of Crewe Alexandra never played

Q: WHO WERE THE FIRST LEAGUE SIDE TO SCORE OVER ONE HUNDRED POINTS IN A SEASON?

without his lucky sock. He always wore it on his right foot under his football sock. Darren believed his right foot was protected and enhanced by the sock. There was a picture of it: it was maroon and a bit tatty.

This was a better superstition. Mike could pursue it in secret and with minimum effort. He could just slip a lucky sock on inside his football pair. Easy!

He just needed a sock. As ever, Mike's clothes were all over the place. He rummaged around on the floor, under the bed, in the wardrobe and through his drawers. He found nothing which inspired him.

Then, hidden away near the bottom of one of his drawers he saw those novelty musical socks he'd got for Christmas. Each one had a red plastic nose which flashed and played "Rudolph the Red-nosed Reindeer" when you pressed it. Would they do? They were dreadful, with the reindeer grinning stupidly on each leg, but nobody would see them. And a lucky sock *should* be a bit unusual. He could use one and roll the other one up in the drawer with all the other clothes he never wore (mostly cardigans). It wouldn't be missed.

He tried on one of the socks for size, under his usual football one. The red plastic nose stuck out a bit, but that would be covered by a shin pad. He put one on and knocked it hard to check that the nose wouldn't dig into his leg. It didn't, but the sock began to flash and play "Rudolph the Red-nosed Reindeer".

This was a design flaw, but it was easily fixed. Mike took the lucky sock off, lifted the nose up and poked the little battery out with his penknife. It fell into the pile of clothes on the floor.

Q: WHO IS THE ONLY ACE MARKSMAN TO HAVE SCORED HAT-TRICKS IN CONSECUTIVE WORLD CUPS?

He tried the combination on again.

It was discreet, soundless and, Mike hoped, lucky.

The Marauders' next game was the first round of the District Cup. All the local teams competed for this and the finals were played at Windley Fields, the County FA's headquarters. They'd been drawn against Vale Rovers, who were down near the bottom of the league with the Marauders. It ought not to be too harsh a test for the newly-appointed lucky sock.

Mike set off for the ground with a spring in his step. Partly because of the extra layer of sock and partly out of confidence that the Marauders were on the threshold of a historic cup-run. As usual, he met Paul on his way to the ground.

"So, Paul. A key cup-tie for the Marauders. Your thoughts?" Mike had put on a John Motson voice and thrust an imaginary microphone under Paul's chin.

"I expect we'll get leathered again. And pack it in, Mike," he said, knocking Mike's hand away.

"Hmm. Confidence low in the Marauders' camp. Let's hope it won't affect their performance," continued Mike Motson.

Mike kept this up all the way to the ground. He was silenced, however, by Mr Harris's team-talk. Mr H had clearly decided that a fresh start was needed for the Marauders' cup-bid. His usual snappy team-talk had been replaced by complex instructions to each player.

The lads sat there puzzled. Paul had a particularly bad time. After baffling everybody with flat back-fours, overlapping wing-halves and tracking-back strikers, Mr Harris turned to Mike's mate.

Q: WHICH PLAYER IS GLASGOW RANGERS' RECORD GOALSCORER IN ALL COMPETITIONS?

"Paul, lad. Today you're going to play in the hole."

"Sorry, Mr Harris?" said Paul.

"You're going to drop off deep behind the two strikers, d'you see?"

"Right."

"Playing in the hole, OK?"

"OK."

None of the team had any idea what this was about, but it was too late for questions. The ref came in to tell them it was time to warm up.

The game started and the Marauders were rampant. At least, they were after they'd all decided to ignore Mr Harris's tactics. Mike's enthusiasm was the inspiration for the whole team. He was on fire.

The Marauders ran out four-nil victors and Mike scored a hat-trick in the first half; each goal an exquisite strike with his right, lucky-socked foot. The plastic nose itched a bit, but the discomfort was worth it.

The post-match celebrations were ecstatic. The team wasn't used to winning. They sang "There's only one Michael Eastman" and "We're on our way to Windley, we shall not be moved".

Mr Harris called for quiet. "Lads. Now you see what can be done. It's a matter of tactics. All you need is a good team shape."

"And Mike Eastman," said Paul, cueing another rendition of "There's only one Michael Eastman".

"Now, Paul. It's not about individuals, d'you see? The team was more mobile out there. Particularly with you in the hole. Oh, yes." Mr Harris looked proudly at his players.

Q: WHAT IS REFEREE PETER WILLIS FAMOUS FOR?

Mike knew that it wasn't anything to do with Paul or the hole or even Mike.

It was the lucky sock.

The league match the following week was postponed because of an icy pitch, so Mike didn't get the chance to give the lucky sock a run-out outside the pressures of a cup-tie. The next outing for the sock would be round two of the Cup, the road to Windley.

Once again, the lucky sock came up trumps. Just one goal for Mike this time (right foot, of course) but two more for his team-mates in a confident, professional three-one victory.

Paul and Mike walked home after the match.

"We're the business now, aren't we?" said Paul.

"Yeah, Cup Kings."

"I can't figure it out. We were bobbins a couple of weeks ago. What's the difference? It's not Harris's weird tactics. Everyone ignores them."

"Can you keep a secret, Paul?" asked Mike.

Mike pulled the lucky sock out of his bag.

"What's that?" Paul asked, appalled.

"Don't laugh, but it's my lucky sock. I've worn this on my right foot for the two cup-ties and I've scored four goals. That's the difference."

"Of course it is," scoffed Paul.

"Well, have you got any better suggestions?"

"What about league matches? It's been years since we won one of those."

"We haven't had any league matches since I started wearing it. Otherwise the magic of the sock would have worked there too."

Q: WHICH LIVERPOOL AND ENGLAND MIDFIELDER IS MARRIED TO POP SINGER LOUISE?

"Oh, for goodness' sake! Well, if you're so sure about this sock, you'd better make sure you wear it next week. It's the quarter-final."

"You bet. Actually, I think I'm only going to wear it in the cup matches. I don't want to wear out the good luck."

Paul rolled his eyes and sighed.

"How d'you get on, Mike?" asked his dad. Mike had just got home from the quarter-final, dumped his football kit in the laundry basket and come downstairs for dinner.

"Four-two," Mike grinned.

"Well done, son," said Dad. "Did you score?"

"Just the one this week," replied Mike, modestly.

Mike's mum was rummaging through the laundry.

"Mike? What's this?" she asked, holding up Rudolph. "It was in one of your football socks. It's one of those you got for Christmas, isn't it?"

"Er, yeah. The football sock had a hole in it. I wore the other one to stop it rubbing."

"Oh, well. I'll fix that." She unrolled the football socks. "There's no holes in these, Mike."

Mum and Dad were both looking at Mike.

"Oh, look, it's my lucky sock, OK?"

"Your what?" asked Dad.

"Whenever I wear it, I score. It's my lucky sock. It's our secret weapon."

"I'd better wash it, then," said his mum, looking a bit alarmed.

* * *

Q: BY WHAT NAME ARE TEACHER'S FC NOW KNOWN?

Next Saturday was the semi-final against Hardgate. As Dad backed the car out of the drive, Mike's mum appeared at the front door, waving. Mike looked at her, wondering what she was up to. He noticed she had a piece of cloth in her hand. It was the lucky sock!

"Dad! Stop! My sock!" Mike screamed.

His dad slammed on the brakes, and Mike was out of the car in a flash. He ran up to his mum, panting with terror.

"You nearly forgot that," she said.

"God, thanks, Mum." Mike grabbed it and ran back to the car. His dad frowned at him and pulled away.

When they reached the ground, Mike ran into the changing room. Mr Harris was running through some new tactics.

"Now, hush up, lads. I'd like to keep things tight across the middle today. Paul, we'll have you as an orthodox midfielder, d'you see?"

Paul looked relieved, but then thought he'd better check.

"So, it's just midfield?"

"Yes."

"So, not in the hole?"

"No."

"Right."

"And David," continued Mr Harris. "Libero. OK?"

David, one of the centre-backs, grimaced and shook his head.

"Sweeper? Play behind the back four?" said Mr Harris, helpfully.

David nodded unconvincingly.

"Good luck, lads. One step from Windley."

Hardgate took an early lead. David was caught at the back, trying to figure out what a "libero" was. But Mike (lucky sock in

Q: WHO IS THE ONLY PLAYER TO HAVE WON THE WORLD PLAYER OF THE YEAR AWARD IN CONSECUTIVE SEASONS?

place) got an equalizer early in the second half (a cheeky back-flick when the ball ran loose after a corner) and hit a screamer from outside the box for the winner. Both with his right foot, of course. The Market Street Marauders would face the Westcott Bees in the final.

Dad gave Mike and Paul a lift home.

"Thank God for the sock," said Mike, as they pulled out of the playing field. Paul cleared his throat.

Mike's dad turned the radio down.

"Mike. Those were two good goals you got out there," he said. "It wasn't the sock. Give yourself some credit."

"It was the sock. I'm rubbish without it. Aren't I, Paul?"

"Well, yeah." Paul had to agree.

"See, Dad, it's my lucky sock."

His dad drove on. Nobody spoke for a while.

"Ha! I'd better remember my lucky sock for the Final," Mike said, out of the blue. "Dread to think what'd happen without it."

Mike's dad sighed and pulled into Paul's road.

"Mum?"

Mike was ringing home from his grandparents'. Grandad had been ill and Mike had been staying there during half-term. It was the eve of the District Cup Final. The twin towers of Windley beckoned.

"I'm going straight to Windley tomorrow for the final. Can you bring my kit?"

"Yes. We'll see you there."

"And Mum?"

"Yes, Mike?"

Q: WHICH SCOTTISH CLUB WOULD YOU FIND AT LOVE STREET?

"Don't forget my lucky sock. It'll be in my wardrobe. Or under the bed."

"No, Mike. We won't forget your lucky sock."

They didn't forget the lucky sock. It's just that when they were getting ready to leave and sorting Mike's kit out, they couldn't find it. His room was a tip, as usual. Dad waded through a sea of clothes.

"June, where's Mike's sock?" he shouted downstairs.

"He said it was in his wardrobe," Mum shouted back.

But it wasn't. Well, he couldn't find it anyway.

Mike didn't take the news well when they got to the ground without his sock.

"Dad. I have to have that sock! I can't play without it. It's kick-off in a few minutes. What am I going to do? This is the CUP FINAL and I don't have my lucky sock!" Mike was nearly hysterical.

"Mike, calm down," said his mum, worried. "I'll go back and look for it again."

"Thanks, Mum. Be quick!"

In the changing room, the lads were in good spirits. Windley's changing rooms were palatial compared to what the lads were used to and a few were mucking around with the hand-dryers and showers. Mr Harris called them to order.

"Now, lads. This is the District Cup Final," he said helpfully. "You know what you've got to do. You've learnt your tactics and they've worked well. I don't need to go over them with you again."

The team breathed a collective, silent sigh of relief.

 **Q:** WHICH CURRENT PREMIERSHIP MANAGER EARNED THE NICKNAME "CAPTAIN MARVEL" DURING HIS PLAYING DAYS?

"Just go out there and enjoy yourselves. Are you OK, Mike?"

Mike was pale and miserable. He was contemplating the loss of his lucky sock and with it, the loss of the District Cup Final.

"I'm fine, Mr Harris."

The lads ran out to cheers. The final had attracted a good turn-out of parents and mates. The ref blew his whistle and the game kicked off.

Mike kept looking out for his mum. The game went on around him.

"Come on, Mike! Get forward!" his dad shouted.

Mike trundled towards the Bees' goal. The ball was played forward and the ref blew his whistle.

"Mike! You're offside. Pay attention!" shouted Mr Harris.

Mike began to look for the ball. A couple of minutes later, it broke to him in space. Mike ran into the area and wound himself up to shoot. He unleashed his right foot, stumbled and kicked the turf behind the ball, which rolled out for a goal kick.

"Unlucky, Mike," said Paul, running up to him. "That took a bit of a bobble."

"It's because I haven't got my sock!" Mike wailed.

Mike missed two more decent chances. Then, not long before half-time, he was through on goal with only the keeper to beat. Somehow, Mike spooned the ball into the keeper's arms. The keeper cleared it downfield to a Bees midfielder, who played it to a striker, who ran in and scored.

This was getting desperate. Where was his sock?

Half-time came and went in a blur for Mike. Mr H tried to buoy the lads up while Mike looked out for his mum's car.

Q: WHO WAS THE FIRST PLAYER IN ENGLISH FOOTBALL TO PLAY 1000 PROFESSIONAL MATCHES?

The second half kicked off. Mike's attention began to wander again. He played a loose ball which was intercepted by the Bees' midfield. They surged forward and scored a second goal.

As the ball was being passed back to the centre spot, Paul ran across to Mike.

"Sort it out, Mike. That was your fault," he said.

"Sorry. I know. Look, my mum'll be here any minute with my sock."

"And does that mean you'll stop playing like a prat?"

Mike had been thinking about how he would be able to put the sock on.

"Paul, when she gets here, give it a couple of minutes and then go down injured. I'll run off and put the sock on."

Paul agreed. The Marauders needed Mike on top of his game and if that was what it took, he'd do it. It didn't look good, though. The Cup Final depended on the arrival of a novelty sock.

As Paul lay on the ground, screaming and clutching his shin, Mike ran off to meet his mum. "Broken shoelace, ref," he shouted as he went.

The ref didn't take any notice because he was preoccupied with Paul. Neither of the linesmen could figure out who was responsible for the devastating foul which had felled this poor lad. The Westcott players shrugged their shoulders. It wasn't any of them. Mr Harris administered the sponge.

Mike sprinted back on to the pitch unnoticed by all but Paul who, to the further puzzlement of the match officials, stopped screaming and got up. Mr Harris couldn't believe what a great physio he was. "Magic sponge," he said proudly to the ref.

 **Q:** WHERE IS THE WORLD'S LARGEST FOOTBALL STADIUM?

Meanwhile, Mike had taken up his position at the front. He felt reborn. He clapped his hands and shouted encouragement to the Marauders.

The ref restarted the game with a drop ball. The Bees returned the ball to the Marauders' goalkeeper (very sporting), who launched it upfield. Mike screamed for the ball. It dropped to the lad playing wide on the right, he crossed it to Mike and Mike controlled it with his chest. He knocked it down to his right foot, now blessed with the lucky sock, and slammed it into the net. The sock had already begun to work. The Marauders were back in the game.

The Bees kicked off, only for the Marauders' midfield to win the ball. Mike's confidence was as infectious as his poor form had been. They knocked the ball around and moved it forward, but Westcott were marking closely and closed the Marauders down. With ten minutes left, they finally broke through. Paul won a tackle on the edge of the box and the ball broke clear to Mike. He made no mistake as he crashed it into the goal. The teams were level.

The Marauders pressed for the winner. There wasn't much time left. The Bees had the ball in midfield. That ball was going to be Mike's. He marauded back and took it off the Westcott player's foot. He ran forward.

The Bees' centre-back, the guy marking Mike, came across to intercept him. Mike drifted wide to the right of the penalty box, but the Bees' defender kept coming. He slid in, studs high, and clattered into Mike's right shin. The ball squirted loose for a throw-in.

Mike lay in agony near the touchline. He screamed and rolled

Q: WHAT DO AC MILAN, BAYERN MUNICH, PARIS ST GERMAIN AND THE IRISH NATIONAL SIDE HAVE IN COMMON?

around as Mr Harris ran to see if he was OK. Not again, thought the ref, lumbering across. He told the players to keep back as he went over to speak to the Westcott defender.

Mike's mum and dad ran over, horrified to see him so brutally felled.

Mike lay there in a daze. The pain was terrible. He couldn't open his eyes. All he could hear was Mr Harris and his mum asking if he was OK. And the sound of music. He must be delirious. The pain began to subside as Mr Harris loosened his boot, but the music continued. Mike could hear it clearly. He even recognized the tune. It was "Rudolph the Red-nosed Reindeer".

"Are you OK, Mike?" asked his mum.

"See if you can move your foot," said Dad.

"What's that music?" said Mr Harris.

Mike's shin seemed to be throbbing. It shone red. Mr Harris was very concerned. He'd never seen anything like this before. He took off Mike's shin-pad and rolled down his sock. A gruesome sight was revealed. It was Rudolph the Red-nosed Reindeer, grinning. His red nose was flashing in time to the music, which was now quite loud.

Mike leant forward. "Mum, where did you get this sock?" he croaked.

"Mike, are you OK, sweetie?" she asked.

"This isn't my lucky sock," he said. "Where did you find it?"

"It was in your cardigan drawer. No wonder we couldn't find it!"

Mike groaned and lay back on the ground. That would teach him not to put his sports kit away properly.

Q: WHO ARE THE BHOYS?

He glanced towards the pitch. The ref had stopped play. He'd put the ball on the penalty spot and was sending off the Westcott player who'd cropped Mike.

Mike's dad took Mike's sock off and pressed the nose to stop the music. Mike eased himself up. He put his weight on his foot. It didn't feel too bad. Mr Harris congratulated himself again on his healing skills.

"I still haven't got my lucky sock," said Mike.

"Forget your lucky sock, Mike!" said his dad. "Look, you got those goals out there without it. If you can do it with all this junk rattling around in your boot –" Mike's dad waved the sock at him – "think what you can do without it. Come on!"

Mike nodded. His dad was right. He'd got the Marauders back into the game without Rudolph. He'd win the game without him too.

He ran on, straight up to the penalty area. The crowd applauded.

"How long left, ref?" asked Mike.

"Minute or two," he said. "Are you OK, son?"

Mike was fine.

Paul and Ian were debating who should take the penalty.

"Stand aside," said Mike, barging past them to the edge of the box. He knew what to do.

"Steady, Mike," said Paul. "That lucky sock doesn't make you Alan Shearer, you know."

"I have no lucky sock," said Mike proudly.

The ref blew his whistle. Mike lined up the kick. The ball was in before he touched it. He ran up and despatched it cleanly into the goal with his right foot. Three-two.

 **Q: WHAT NICKNAME DO LUTON TOWN AND STOCKPORT COUNTY SHARE?**

Mike was mobbed by the Marauders. The ref had to break it up so the Bees could kick-off.

They knew it was over. There was less than a minute to go. The Marauders won possession and kept it. They stroked the ball around and the little clump of Marauders fans cheered every time a Marauder touched it.

The ref blew for time. The Marauders had won the District Cup. They were the Kings of Windley.

They shook hands with the Westcott players. Paul was the first to congratulate Mike. Then they were swept up by the other Marauders for the victory photograph and the presentation.

Mr Harris was arranging the lads into rows. He was making a big fuss, moving everyone around.

Paul shouted, "Mr Harris, where would you like me for the photo? In the hole?"

The Market Street Marauders, holders of the District Cup, roared with laughter.

Quiz Answers

The New Kid

p41 He was the first professional to score hat-tricks on three consecutive Saturdays. Portsmouth, Derby and Arsenal were the unwary 1946 opponents.

p42 Arsenal.

p43 Pickles (a collie) found the stolen Jules Rimet trophy in his front garden on 20th March 1966.

p44 Exeter City and Newcastle United.

p45 Dennis Bergkamp.

p46 Belgium. They managed a 2–2 draw in a 1923 friendly.

p48 Everton – during 1958–59. It cost £70,000 and didn't work.

p49 Manchester City.

p50 Vinnie Jones. He was booked after just three seconds of a match against Sheffield United.

p51 Notts County.

p52 Macclesfield Town.

p53 Michel Platini.

p54 White Hart Lane

Fantasy Football

p59 England's Geoff Hurst in 1966.

p60 Kevin Keegan (Liverpool and Hamburg) and Frank Gray (Leeds and Nottingham Forest).

p61 Ian Rush.

p62 Ian Rush.

p63 Newcastle.

p64 Lothar Matthaus.

p65 Nottingham Forest.

p66 Leeds United.

p67 Manchester United. They planted nine past the unfortunate Ipswich Town in 1995.

p68 Real Madrid.

p69 Reading.

p71 Lincoln City.

Mike's Lucky Sock

p75 Roma and Lazio.

p76 John Motson.

p77 Johan Cruyff and Marco Van Basten.

p78 York City notched up 101 in 1983–84.

p79 Argentina's Gabriel Batistuta.

p80 Ally McCoist.

p81 He was the first ref to dismiss a player during an FA Cup Final.

p82 Jamie Redknapp.

p83 Sunderland.

p84 Ronaldo.

p85 St Mirren.

p86 Brian Robson.

p87 Peter Shilton.

p88 The Maracana in Rio de Janeiro, Brazil.

p89 They are all sponsored by the car company Opel.

p91 Celtic.

p92 The Hatters.

Following Pompey

Dennis Hamley

Dennis Hamley has written many stories, about football, ghosts, murders, wars, trains and animals – sometimes all at once. He contributed *Proud Preston* to the NICE ONE, SANTA! anthology.

Dennis has always supported Pompey, but excuses himself with the thought that, when he was nobbut a lad, they were great! One day they will be again. You'll see!

Things weren't going well for Ross and St Alfred's under-thirteens, and he was worried. Two defeats and a draw when they were going for the league wasn't the stuff of champions.

Today against Birtlesbury was typical. It was the last game but two of the season. All over them in the first half, red-and-black striped shirts pouring down on the Birtlesbury goal, their beanpole goalkeeper shaking at his knobbly knees. They hit post, bar, put the ball wide, over, into the side-netting. Danny Drew's penalty amazingly hit the goalkeeper on the head then bounced out while he was looking round to see what had happened. Danny was so surprised that he missed his kick at the rebound and Birtlesbury cleared it. Ross himself had the ball at his feet five metres in front of an empty net and still put it wide. He knew he'd have nightmares about that for weeks. Birtlesbury were so relieved they scored straight from the goal kick and in the second half packed their goal so a squadron of Challenger tanks wouldn't have got through.

With only two matches to go now and other teams chasing them hard, what chance did they have?

In fact, football was gloomy everywhere at the moment. The Premiership team he supported was on the slide as well. It was as if there were disasters wherever he looked. That evening he talked about it when Uncle Cyril and Aunt Freda came round to their house.

Q: WHICH POP STAR'S UNCLE SCORED A GOAL AND BROKE HIS LEG IN THE 1959 CUP FINAL?

In age, Uncle Cyril was knocking on a bit. He was nearly twenty years older than Dad – but then Aunt Freda was fifteen years older than Mum, her sister. They'd been oldest and youngest in a large family. "I was a brilliant afterthought," Mum said. "Unfortunate accident, you mean," said Dad when he was feeling sour with the world.

Ross liked Uncle Cyril, in spite of his uncool name. He came from the other end of the country and his voice had an unfamiliar burr to it. Like all the men in the family – and the women too, if it came to that – Cyril was crackers about football. When he was a boy he'd played to a pretty high level and might have gone a long way – until the accident which left him with a permanent limp.

Anyway, Ross knew Uncle Cyril would ask about his team and he wished he had the usual tales of success. He certainly planned to keep quiet about missing that goal.

Only he didn't. Something about Uncle Cyril meant he didn't mind telling him awkward things. He always seemed to have the right answer. Although, this time, as Cyril began to speak, Ross wasn't so sure. . .

"That lot you fancy in the Premiership haven't done so well either, have they?" Uncle Cyril said.

"Don't rub it in," Ross replied.

Uncle Cyril wouldn't be checked. "There's a funny thing in life that I've always found true," he said. "If your team's doing well, things go brilliantly in life for you. But if your team's not, then ... well, life's not so rosy either—"

"That's a big help," Ross interrupted. "You're *really* cheering me up, Uncle Cyril."

 **Q:** WHICH PRIME MINISTER'S SON HAD A TRIAL FOR ASTON VILLA?

"Hold on, I haven't finished. If you don't know what I'm going to say next, you're not a true football supporter."

Ross didn't answer. What did he mean, not a true football supporter?

"Ah, you're puzzled. I'll put it this way. Suppose your top-flight darlings get relegated? Will you find someone else to support?"

Ross was appalled at the suggestion. "Never!" he answered.

"That's good," said Uncle Cyril. "That's what I mean. Stick by them – and by St Alfred's – and it'll all come good in the end. There's more to football than just one season. Look at Manchester City. You can laugh now, but I remember them winning League, Cup and Cup-Winners Cup in successive seasons. Their supporters remember as well. They know City will come back. They'll be patient and wait. That's what I call the *true* supporters, the *real* ones."

Ross felt a stab of guilt. If his team *did* go down – well, he often envied his mates who followed United or Arsenal. So he said, a bit spitefully, "I bet your team will never come back. I bet they weren't there in the first place."

"Portsmouth?" said Uncle Cyril. "Don't you believe it."

Ross looked at Uncle Cyril. As a boy he'd spent his childhood in Portsmouth, because his father had been in the Navy. That accounted not only for his Hampshire accent but also his love of Pompey, even though he lived miles away now.

As if he knew what Ross was thinking, he said, "Yes, I know things aren't too good at the moment. I wish I lived nearer so I could join in the Pompey Chimes again."

Ross sniffed scornfully.

Q: WHICH CLUB WAS PROMOTED TO DIVISION ONE, RELEGATED TO DIVISION THREE, THEN FINISHED UP STAYING IN DIVISION TWO – ALL AT THE END OF THE 1990–91 SEASON?

"It would be no worse than watching your lot," said Uncle Cyril. "And at least you get a chance to see them. They're on satellite TV on Sunday, aren't they?"

Yes, they were. Big relegation battle. Ross wondered how he could bring himself to watch it. If they lost...

"If you really support them, you'll watch every second and live every kick," said Uncle Cyril.

Ross shivered slightly. It was the first leg of an end-of-season double: the Premiership match on Sunday, then St Alfred's crunch game on Monday evening. If the first leg went wrong when he watched, what disaster might happen in the second when he played?

That Sunday they were all in front of the television – Ross, Dad, Uncle Cyril, even Mum and Aunt Freda. It was terrible. "Gutless, witless lot," scoffed Dad. "They're a disgrace to their shirts." When the final whistle blew, Ross's team had gone down three-nil at home. Following United or Arsenal next season seemed very attractive.

Uncle Cyril smiled sympathetically. "You don't choose your football team," he said. "They choose you. And don't worry. They aren't down yet."

Not down yet? When they needed three points to stay in the Premiership next week and were away to a team pushing for Europe? It looked pretty hopeless to Ross. And in twenty-four hours came that last but one St Alfred's match against Wington Youth. If they lost that they'd have a mountain to climb too. How had everything got this bad?

* * *

 **Q:** NAME THE ONLY COUNTRY NOT TO LOSE A MATCH IN THE 1974 WORLD CUP FINALS.

St Alfred's had a ground down by the river. Ross loved it, especially when, for most of the season, it was an arena of triumph. The red and black shirts had swept aside everything – until this last month.

It was a pleasant, sunny, end-of-season evening. Wington weren't a bad outfit, but St Alfred's started off as if they'd put everything to rights that had gone wrong recently. Ross felt there was purpose and determination about them. Scott Briggs in defence brought the ball away, slipped it out to Danny Drew and Danny's cross dropped beautifully to Ross's feet. The Wington defender came sliding over but Ross dummied past with all the assurance he'd felt for the first months of the season. He had a perfect sight of goal and plenty of time. He could pick his spot. Bottom left-hand corner. He sidefooted his careful, measured shot with the goalkeeper nowhere to be seen and turned away, arms raised.

Except that he hadn't quite measured it right. The ball slid an inch the wrong side of the post and went for a goal kick.

A month ago, it would have been, "Unlucky, Ross. There's four more where that came from." Now it was all: "You daft twit. Watch what you're doing, can't you?" That first ten minutes was a false dawn. St Alfred's went to pieces. Wington went home four-nil winners.

Complete disaster. Both Parkerton and St Olave's, their nearest rivals, won that evening. St Alfred's were now a point behind both. It really looked as if both legs of Ross's end-of-season double were knocked away. Relegation for one: no championship for the other.

Unless there was a miracle.

Q: WHO WON EURO '92 DESPITE FAILING TO QUALIFY FOR THE FINAL STAGES?

"Miracles can happen," said Uncle Cyril. "Especially in football. As many miracles as disasters. That's the faith of the football supporter."

"More disasters than miracles when you follow Pompey," said Ross.

"I don't know so much," Uncle Cyril replied. He was quiet for a moment, then he said, "Let me tell you a story."

"If you want," said Ross. "Though I don't see how stories can help."

"Well, this may do," said Uncle Cyril. "I wasn't yet ten when I got interested in football. Caught it from my dad first. Well, living in Portsmouth, it had to be Pompey. Not that I got to see them much, what with Dad being away in the navy such a lot and my mother hating the game and not letting me go on my own. I thought she was a bit mean. She wouldn't let me go with any-body else either. Said one shilling and threepence was far too much to pay to watch grown men chase a scrap of leather round the field. He stopped and smiled to himself. "Honestly," he said. "Women!"

Ross waited. Uncle Cyril seemed lost in a world of his own for a second. Then he started again. "Anyway," he said. "The first match Dad took me to was the day before he went to sea for a long while. He was in destroyers and they were going out to Aden and the Indian Ocean for a long tour of duty. I remember the game too. Pompey were in the old First Division then and it was their Golden Jubilee year: fifty years since they were found-ed. Everybody thought it would be great to be champions to mark it, but I don't think anyone really thought they'd manage it. Not to start with anyway. But when Dad took me along to

Q: WHICH PLAYER HOLDS THE RECORD FOR THE MOST GOALS SCORED IN A PREMIERSHIP MATCH?

Fratton Park that first time, there were Pompey, still top of the league in April, at home to Liverpool, and everybody saying: 'Can they really do it?' It was a great game. Pompey went in two-nil up at half-time and it looked like it was going to be easy. But they had to scramble to nick it three-two in the end and there were a lot of relieved people walking down the Milton Road afterwards. Pompey weren't going to falter now, were they?

"Ah, but the next match in midweek was against Newcastle up at St James's. The Magpies were going well: they still had a shout in the championship. Sixty thousand turned up, so the papers said, because it was a real crunch game. And what do you think? Pompey came away five-nil winners. Hat-trick for Jack Froggatt and two for Peter Harris – the two flying wingers. Every goal was headed. That's style for you. Seems hard to believe it today. Everyone knew nobody could stop them now. A fortnight later they beat Bolton at dear old Burnden Park and they were champions. It's a pity there was no European Cup then. I wonder how they'd have done.

"By that time Dad was on the other side of the world, but he wrote me a letter to celebrate. 'When I come home, we'll go to watch the game when Pompey clinch next year's title,' he said.

"I was only a little kid then. It never dawned on me that that might be anything but an absolute promise. They were going to do it. He'd said so, so it would happen. And then Dad would stay home for good, because he was leaving the Navy when he got back."

Uncle Cyril was quiet again, this time for a few moments. Ross waited. When Cyril finally spoke he seemed to have changed the subject. "Remember what I said about things going well when

Q: WHICH COUNTRY QUALIFIED FOR THE 1958 WORLD CUP FINALS AS REPRESENTATIVES OF ASIA-AFRICA?

your team's doing well and badly when they're not?" Ross nodded. "Well, when I came off my motorbike, broke this –" he patted his bad leg – "and it never set right, it was the season Pompey were first relegated to the Second Division. The year my dad, your great-uncle Sid, died was the year Pompey went down to the Fourth Division."

Ross stared and he felt a cold shiver. Did that mean...?

Uncle Cyril seemed to read his thoughts. "No, I don't mean those things happened *because* they were relegated. I rode my motorbike like an idiot and Dad had been ill for a long time. They'd have happened if Pompey had done the Double each year. And we wouldn't have avoided them by supporting Spurs instead. No, it's just strange how disasters happen together. There were no miracles then."

Another silence. Then: "Those ships should have been home well before next season ended. But this was the Cold War. Things were dodgy between the West and Russia. Britain was getting rid of its Empire. We were giving independence to countries all through Africa. India and Pakistan had got rid of us a couple of years before. But there were some places we were hanging on to because of the oil and because we'd got big bases for the army and air force in them and the people who really lived there were fed up with us. There was trouble brewing. It was soon clear Dad's destroyer wouldn't be home when it was supposed to be. So he couldn't leave the navy when he was meant to.

"When the next season started, it soon looked like Pompey had no chance of keeping the title. In the first four games they got beaten by Newcastle, Blackpool and Manchester City and

Q: WHICH SIDE PLAYS THEIR HOME MATCHES AT THE AMSTERDAM ARENA?

only managed a draw against City again. It looked more like relegation form. Well, they beat Middlesborough five-one, who weren't much cop that year, but two days later they went down to Aston Villa so it was still gloomy. And then they had Everton at home and, would you believe, they beat them seven-nil. Yes, *seven-nil*! That turned the corner all right. After that, Huddersfield, Birmingham, Derby and Chelsea all bit the dust and Pompey were there or thereabouts at the top – and there they stayed. And I never saw a single ball kicked!

"Every week we got a letter from Dad and he always wrote about Pompey's latest match. There he was, five thousand miles away, and he knew as much about what was happening as I did. Round about February they had a wobble. Bolton, Wolves and Derby beat them and they had a nasty time in the fifth round of the Cup. They drew three-three at Old Trafford but then United took them two-one at Fratton. It seemed their heads had definitely gone down. And still Dad was stuck miles away. The Cup had gone and the League was slipping away, but I didn't worry – Dad had made me a promise and I knew he'd keep it.

"April passed, May came. His destroyer was still out in Aden. He was supposed to be leaving the navy the next week. There were only four games to go and at least four teams with a chance of the title. Pompey went back to Old Trafford and this time beat United two-nil. Then they won two-one at Anfield. They were equal top with Wolves. Two matches to go. First, midweek, away to Arsenal. If they won, they'd be champions. But Dad didn't come home and I knew what would happen. Sixty-five thousand people jammed inside Highbury and Pompey went down two-nil.

Q: FOR WHAT AMAZING FEAT IS TRANMERE ROVERS' ROBERT "BUNNY" BELL FAMED?

"No chance now, I thought. I said to Mum: 'He will be home in time for Saturday, won't he?' I can still see her pitying look. 'How fast do you think ships can sail, Cyril?' she said. Well, that was it, wasn't it? Forget it. If Wolves beat Birmingham and Pompey only drew, then Wolves would be champions by one point and, since Birmingham were already relegated, what chance had they at Molineux?

"Pompey were playing Aston Villa at Fratton, and Villa were a good side that season. It looked like there was a Midlands conspiracy to do Pompey out of a second championship. And the navy weren't helping, keeping my dad away so he couldn't keep his promise. No Dad, no championship, that's how I saw it.

"I didn't want to know. I wouldn't listen to the wireless or read the papers – as far as I was concerned, Pompey were beaten. If I wasn't there with Dad then they had no chance.

"I was in a terrible state. I'd been so sure everything would work out the way Dad said, and now it hadn't. I couldn't eat anything Mum put in front of me. 'You're not well,' she said. 'It's bed for you.' And, do you know, I couldn't care less. Twelve o'clock came, one o'clock. The crowds would be streaming into Fratton Park by then, the South Stand and the Fratton End would be filling, the crowd would be tuning up with a few efforts at the Pompey Chimes – and they were wasting their money, time and breath. Pompey wouldn't win, I just knew it."

He paused again. Then he said, "You see, Ross, it was like it is for you now. Two things going wrong together. Pompey losing the league and Dad not being back for me; for you, the team you support being relegated and the team you play for missing out."

"Yes," said Ross. "I see. So did you have a miracle?"

Q: WHICH PLAYER HOLDS THE RECORD FOR THE MOST GOALS SCORED IN AN ENGLISH LEAGUE CAMPAIGN?

Uncle Cyril smiled and went on. "I got into bed and closed my eyes. Perhaps I dozed off. And then I heard a knock at the door. 'Who can that be?' I heard Mum say as she went to open it. I heard her gasp and then give a little joyful scream. I got out of bed and went downstairs to see who it was – and there was Dad, in his sailor's hat and his bell bottoms, his kitbag over his shoulder, saying, 'Well, I made it in time. After all, a promise is a promise. I've got a couple of tickets for this afternoon. Aren't you ready yet, Cyril?'"

Uncle Cyril stopped again and smiled to himself. "I'll never forget that moment as long as I live."

Another short silence, then he went on. "I never bothered to ask how he'd got there. He'd come like he said he would, that's what mattered. Besides, I was sure I was dreaming. Now it only remained for Pompey to keep their side of the bargain. After all, he'd said he'd be there when they clinched their next championship, so they'd have to do it. But I still didn't fancy their chances.

"We scrambled on to a bus and just before kick-off we were pushing our way up the Frogmore Road, past the Pompey pub and under the half-timbered gateway looking like some Elizabethan mansion. We showed our tickets and I found myself in the front row of the upper deck of the main South Stand, best view in the place. How had Dad managed to wangle such seats? The teams were just coming out. Villa were in claret and blue, Pompey in their royal blue shirts, white shorts and red socks. The team wasn't at its strongest. No Jimmy Scoular: he'd been suspended. No Ike Clarke: he was injured. So that was the strong ball-winner in midfield who never let anything past him and the

Q: WHICH IS BRITAIN'S OLDEST FOOTBALL GROUND?

striker who'd been deadly all season, both out. Still, Bill Spence was a good half-back and Bill Thompson could play anywhere. He'd played centre half for twelve games that season.

"What a sight it was. A lovely sunny day, Fratton packed with fifty thousand fans – you'll never see *that* again. Radios tuned in to catch news of the Wolves game. And me saying to myself: 'Dad's kept his side of the promise so they'll *do* it.'

"Well, it looked like they would. Not half a minute had gone before Bill Thompson, converted defender, stuck the ball in the net. Fratton went wild. Dad jumped up, hugged me and everyone else within reach. Then came the news – Jesse Pye had scored for Wolves. And so it went on. Big Duggie Reid got another by half-time: we went in two-nil up. But Wolves were five-nil up and everyone started thinking about the goals. It was goal average which settled ties on points in those days, not goal difference, and people were furiously calculating all over the ground. What happened if Villa got one back and Wolves got another five? Well, Pompey came out as if that wouldn't happen. Villa did pull one back, but Thompson got another and Duggie Reid finished his hat-trick. So it was five-one to Wolves' six-one and Pompey were champions again because they'd only let thirty-eight goals in all season so their average was much better.

"It was still like a dream. I kept on thinking I'd wake up at any moment. It took ages to get home because we couldn't get through the crowds cheering and dancing in the streets and then we couldn't get on a bus. So it was only when we were nearly home that I realized it wasn't a dream, that Dad was really there and Pompey were really champions again. I looked at him like I

Q: WHO WAS THE FIRST PLAYER TO WIN THE COVETED EUROPEAN GOLDEN BOOT AWARD?

hadn't seen him before. 'Dad,' I said. 'How did you get here?' 'I never thought I'd thank the navy for anything,' he answered. 'But they came up trumps this time. My captain knew I was due out but that the squadron would be stuck in the Gulf for months yet. So he wangled me a seat on an RAF flight from Aden back to Britain. And then he asked if there was anything I'd like before I went as a reward for good service. Two tickets for today, I told him. Bit of a joke, really. Next day he told me to call in at the ground when I got back. So I did, this morning. And there they were, waiting for me. It was all so sudden I never had a chance to let you know. So there you are. I kept my promise and so did Pompey.' "

Cyril stopped talking again and looked out of the window as if he might see once again his father coming up the road in blue bell-bottoms with a kitbag over his shoulder. Then he pulled himself back into the world of the moment. "So that's what I mean," he said. "Football's about disasters and miracles. And the miracles can happen to you as much as to the players themselves."

"Yes, but you can't *make* miracles happen," said Ross.

"Can't you?" said Uncle Cyril. "Well, I'll tell you this. I was so sure Dad would be back and he and Pompey together would keep their promise, that I reckon the force of my certainty *made* the navy put him on the plane and get him the tickets."

"That's daft, Uncle Cyril," said Ross.

"Prove it," Uncle Cyril answered.

"All right," said Ross. "I'm certain my team won't be relegated and I know we're going to win our league. Is that good enough?"

"It is if you mean it," said Uncle Cyril.

 **Q:** WHY DID JIMMY "THE CHIN" HILL DRAMATICALLY EXIT THE COMMENTARY BOX DURING A 1972 ARSENAL–LIVERPOOL MATCH?

* * *

St Alfred's were playing their last game on Monday evening. If they lost, the championship was gone. If they won and Parkerton and St Olave's both lost, they'd have made it after all.

But before that came that vital last Premiership game away to the European hopefuls. Ross tried hard to keep away from radio and television all Sunday. No way did he want to know the result until Match of the Day came on. Then, whatever it was, he could live through it properly. It seemed an eternity before he was sitting in front of the TV and Gary Lineker was saying "...one of those games on which so much depends. For one team, Premiership survival, for the other, a future in Europe." And out they came, while Ross sat at home, gritting his teeth and holding his breath.

The start was awful. "Gutless, witless," Dad had said last week – and today they were worse. Two-nil down at half-time. Ross wondered if they could even survive next season in Division One. "So much for hoping for miracles, Uncle Cyril," he said.

Uncle Cyril smiled. "Like I told you, there are as many miracles as disasters."

The second half started. What a change! It seemed as if his team had been listening to Cyril. They were new men. They were inspired. They set about their opponents as if the points would win the league, not just keep them in it. Three minutes went by: they pulled one goal back. Ten more minutes: the equalizer. Five minutes later: they took the lead. Then they plonked in two more for good measure before the final whistle blew, leaving Alan Hansen and Trevor Brooking muttering about "the greatest escape act since Houdini".

Q: WHICH FAMOUS PARISIAN SIDE PLAYS AT THE PARC DES PRINCES?

"Escape act nothing," said Ross. "They'll be champions next year."

Next day, though, things were different. This wasn't like watching from miles away. This outcome was in their own hands.

They were playing Winsley Youth. After ten minutes it seemed St Alfred's were carrying on from where they left off last Monday. Two-nil down already. "What did your dad say about being gutless and witless?" Uncle Cyril shouted at Ross. "*Believe* in the miracle."

Yes, thought Ross. The young Cyril had had faith, and following Pompey had brought about a great miracle for him, so maybe there *is* something in it. Perhaps it wasn't too late today.

The ball came to him. He collected it, then set off at a run. All right, I *will* have a bit of faith, he thought. A defender blocked his path. He shimmied past. Another tried to slide him. He skipped over his leg. He was on his own. He'd have to do it all himself. A huge central defender loomed up. I can do it, Ross thought. He nutmegged him. "Cheeky!" he heard Uncle Cyril shout. The goalkeeper rushed out, blocking Ross's sight of goal. There was only one thing to do. He lay back and chipped the ball over the goalkeeper's head. Despite a floundering turn and desperate dive, the goalkeeper was nowhere near it. Ross had pulled one back for St Alfred's.

He rushed back to the centre. "We *can* come back. We *can* beat them," he yelled. "Believe it."

His example and message seemed to give an electric shock to the whole team. Now no ball was too hopeless to chase. They

Q: WHO ARE THE INDOMITABLE LIONS?

piled into the Winsley goal. Before half-time, the equalizer came; two minutes into the second half they took the lead. Just like on Match of the Day last night.

But this is no good if Parkerton or St Olave's win as well, Ross thought. And then – They won't. I'm as certain about that as Uncle Cyril was that his dad would come back and Pompey would be champions.

The fourth and last goal was Ross's. A long clearance found Danny Drew who pushed it to Ross, unmarked outside the penalty area. And Ross hit it with one of those perfect, sweet shots that he would remember all his life as it arrowed cleanly off his boot into the net. That's it, he thought. We've done it.

The final whistle blew. Mobile phones were going all round the pitch. Then: "I don't believe it," someone shouted. "Parkerton lost and so did St Olave's. Incredible. You've won the league!"

Amid the joy, Ross went over to Uncle Cyril, who clapped him round the shoulders. "I'm pleased for you, Ross," he said. "Now you really know what the true football supporter goes through."

"I know," shouted Ross delightedly. "Triumph and disaster. And waiting for a miracle."

"Dead right," said Uncle Cyril. "And you certainly get them all through following Pompey."

Pratt's Dad

Haydn Middleton

For Rocky Mitford,
with season's greetings

Haydn Middleton was born in Reading, and for that reason alone he has supported Reading FC since 1964. He now lives in Oxford with his two children, and makes them support Reading too. When not playing, watching or reading about football, he writes about it. Check out his COME AND HAVE A GO series, available from Scholastic.

PRESS RELEASE ISSUED TO ALL
NATIONAL NEWSPAPERS
10.03 AM 17 JANUARY
ALL RIGHTS RESERVED

My name is Jermaine Torso, as I'm sure all you gentlemen of the press know by now. There's not much more to say. I'm still at school. I've got an average number of spots for my age. I quite like Bon Jovi. Oh, and two seasons ago I scored seven goals for my school's reserve team. But I guess you really want me to talk about the Pratts, right? Ron and Gavin. Well there's not a whole lot I can say there, either. But here goes:

It all started three years back. Gavin Pratt came to our school after moving up from Plymouth. He was in my class and we got quite friendly but he was only there for a couple of months. Most people didn't mind him. He wasn't much good at sport but he had a neat twenty-one-gear bike and he could do a slightly disturbing impression of Kate Winslet in *Titanic*.

The only time I ever went to his house, his dad was sitting at the kitchen table with his head in his hands. For a while we ignored him while Pratt's mum made a pot of tea and chatted about how she still missed the West Country. Apparently she'd lived there all her life. Then she nodded at her husband and said,

Q: WHO IS THE WORLD'S MOST CAPPED
INTERNATIONAL PLAYER?

"He's terribly upset because he's just been sold to Nottingham Forest."

"Forest?" I asked. "But they're not such a bad club, are they?"

"Well, no," Pratt's mum answered with a smile. "But that's not really the point. You see, Mr Pratt isn't a footballer. He works in a bank. Barclays. He's usually on the Foreign Exchange counter."

I didn't know if this was a wind-up or what. Then Pratt's dad looked at me and started shaking his head. It was a weird sort of head back then: big and bald and sort of rubbery – like a baby's, only with a gingery-grey moustache and huge horn-rimmed glasses.

"There's been a major mix-up somewhere along the line," he told me. "But I've got to see this as a challenge. Attitude counts for so much. In this day and age you have to be able to adapt, as you lads will be discovering for yourselves soon enough." He took a deep sigh and thanked his wife when she gave him his tea. "There's no such thing as a job for life any more."

Pratt's mum put a hand on his hunched shoulder. "And it could be worse, couldn't it?" she asked. "I mean, at least we know the rules of football. We don't have to start from scratch. And the club is being very generous. We're going up to Nottingham this weekend to look at the house they've found for us."

Once they'd moved, I suppose I thought I'd never see them again. But two months later Pratt rang and invited me to come and stay for half-term. I wasn't sure about going. As I say, I didn't know him all that well. But I went anyway, mainly because I was so sick of doing Science revision for my mock GCSEs.

 **Q:** CAN YOU NAME THE ONLY TWO CLUBS TO HAVE APPEARED IN EVERY FA CUP COMPETITION?

The house they had in Nottingham was really nice. Big and modern – much better than the one they'd lived in before. Pratt's dad was in full training but he hadn't even broken into the reserve team. Some of the fans were starting to grumble. He'd cost the club £225,000 and he still hadn't played a single game in Forest's red and white.

"It's going to happen though, Jermaine," he said to me in their new fitted kitchen. He certainly looked slimmer after all the training; he even seemed to be growing back some of his hair. "It's simply a matter of time now."

But time didn't seem to be on his side. He had just turned forty-two and most footballers start to think of packing it in about ten years *before* that. I didn't know quite how to put this, but it had been preying on my mind for weeks. "Aren't you a bit – um – mature for a new career in football?" I finally asked.

"You're as young as you feel, Jermaine," Pratt's mum cut in, pinching her husband's babyish cheek and grinning. "To me, Mr Pratt is still the same bright-eyed, bushy-tailed youngster that I married twenty years ago. He's just got to convince the Forest manager that he's still in his prime."

That was easier said than done. On my last afternoon I went to the ground with Pratt to watch his dad practice all on his own. After a while I had to stop looking and went for a kick around in the other goal. I mean, I'm not exactly Kevin Keegan and I'm aware that my technique is lacking in certain respects, but Pratt's dad was woeful. Never mind ball skills, there were times when he seriously seemed to have forgotten how to run. As he dragged himself off the pitch at the end, a voice boomed

Q: WHO WERE THE FIRST WINNERS OF THE WORLD CUP?

over the PA system: "Come to the manager's office, Pratt. And take your boots off first."

He was inside for fifteen minutes. When he came out he had a strange look on his face. It took him a while to put his glasses back on. Obviously something big had happened but you couldn't tell if he was happy about it or not.

"What did he say, Dad?" asked Pratt. "Was it the call-up?" (I have to say that in my limited experience of the Pratts, Gavin was always a totally supportive son. He never lost belief in his dad, never doubted his destiny in the game.)

Pratt's dad scratched his head and blinked. "Not exactly," he replied. "Another club appears to be interested in me. They want me on a month's loan, with a view to a permanent transfer."

"Why?" I couldn't help asking, even though this wasn't very polite.

"It's a funny old game, Jermaine," was all he said.

"But you've only been here two months," I went on. For some reason this was bugging me. "You've hardly settled in, and now you're off again."

"In football," Pratt's dad sighed, "you're only ever as good as your last game."

"Or in your case, your last training session," Pratt added earnestly. "But who's come in for you? Which club is it?"

"Ayr United."

"Ayr United?" echoed Pratt, widening his eyes. "So we're off to Wales?"

"Er – Scotland," I corrected him. Pratt hadn't been a high-flier at our school and clearly his Geography hadn't got any

Q: IN WHAT YEAR DID THE FIRST WOMEN'S FA CUP FINAL TAKE PLACE?

better in Nottingham. "Well, good luck, Mr Pratt," I said as I left, and I couldn't help tacking on a little fib, just to make him feel a bit better: "I'm sure it will all come right for you in the end."

He looked at me oddly. For a minute I thought he was going to have a go. But then he beamed, as if I was his long-lost son or something. "Attitude counts for so much, Jermaine," he said. "Thanks a lot for your positive input. I *really* appreciate it. And from what I saw of you kicking around over there, you've got real talent too. Talent and attitude – that's some combination!"

Two weeks later I read about his transfer on the Ayr United website. Forest made a heavy loss on the deal. They sold Pratt's dad on for just £27,500 – plus £2000 more for every goal he scored *plus* (a bit optimistically, I thought) a further £14,000 if he was ever capped at international level.

For the rest of the season I kept an eye on Ayr's results. They didn't have a vintage year. And Pratt's dad didn't appear in any of the line-ups they printed in the papers I looked at. But Scotland was too far away for me just to drop in on the family. Again, I guess I thought we were drifting apart. Then Pratt rang.

"It hasn't been the happiest of moves," he said, with just a trace of a Scottish accent now. "Scotland's a lovely place, and the standard of football up here is lower than in England, but it's still not quite low enough for dad. So when the new offer came, he really didn't think twice about accepting it."

"New offer?" I didn't know anything about this. "What new offer?"

 **Q:** WHO IS THE ONLY ENGLAND PLAYER TO WIN THE WORLD CUP GOLDEN BOOT AWARD?

"To be player-coach of Stal Mielec. It's in eastern Europe somewhere. Hungary I think, or was it the Czech Republic? One of those places."

Poland, actually. I'd heard of them. They were a proper club – or at least they used to be. "So your dad's not bothered about the language barrier?" I asked.

"Not at all," Pratt said confidently. "Nor is the club. They're sure he's the man they need to get them into Europe next season. They believe that his experience in banking will help him to wheel and deal in the transfer market."

What could I say? I just wished them luck again. And I'll admit that I did feel a bit miffed as well. There didn't appear to be anything very special about Pratt's family but they kept on getting these big breaks. Pratt was seeing the world while all I ever seemed to do was revise for Science tests which, by and large, I then failed. "So when are you leaving?" I asked.

"Dad's already on his way. Mum and I will be voyaging out on Friday."

"Voyaging?"

"By trawler. At the present time the club doesn't have a great deal of cash to throw around," Pratt explained. "But we're prepared to rough it a bit. Dad sees it as a kind of crusade – a chance for him to put something back into the game."

When I put down the phone, I was sure that was the last I'd hear. To be honest, I pretty well forgot about Stal Mielec and the Pratts. I had my own life to lead, and plenty of my own Science tests to fail. Then, last December, as if we need reminding now, the England manager was shown the door.

Q: WHICH IS EUROPE'S BIGGEST FOOTBALL STADIUM?

Naturally Pratt's dad wasn't on anyone's shortlist as a possible replacement. All the usual old suspects were, though. Robson, Venables, Ferguson – even Glenn Hoddle got a namecheck. But when the 6/4 favourite declared that he "wouldn't touch that ultimate hiding-to-nothing with a fifty-foot bargepole", he was speaking for everyone else in the running as well.

What happened next is, of course, already a modern football legend. Every "expert" from Bob Wilson to the bloke who collects up the trolleys at our Tesco's started saying that the national team needed a new kind of coach. Someone who knew the game as it was being played beyond these backward shores. A man drawn from the red-hot crucible of technically-advanced European soccer.

For many people, the words *Stal Mielec* were heard for the first time. And, after a slow start, they were heard increasingly often. Then the sports pages were all running photos of the now-slimline, goatskin-coated ex-banker jetting in to meet the media at Heathrow before heading on to Lancaster Gate for his interview with the FA.

KING-ELECT! the headlines were already proclaiming. But it didn't turn out to be much of an election. For that, you needed more than one candidate and no one else could be found to stand against him. So, just a week before Christmas, Ronald Ian Pratt, my mate's dad, was given the biggest job in British football.

"I'm proud, thrilled and amazed," Pratt's dad beamed at the press conference as he buffed up his glasses. "I believe that this can be the start of a whole new era. And I say this in all sincerity – I won't leave my post until I have fully completed the job that I have been appointed to do." Two days later he was sacked. **RIP – RON IAN PRATT!** screamed the tabloids.

Q: WHICH PREDATORY TEAM WOULD YOU FIND AT MOLINEUX?

They had done their homework on the new England supremo – even if they'd handed it in slightly late. The awful truth was laid bare for all to see. Ron Pratt had never kicked a ball cleanly in his life. Never played in a competitive game. Never, it was whispered, even *watched* one all the way through. And, perhaps most damagingly of all, he had worked full-time in a bank till he was forty-one.

Christmas came and went with Pratt's dad in protective custody. No one was quite sure how he should be prosecuted. Some of the suggestions were just crazy – like that Radio One campaign to make him watch old videos of England penalty shootouts for the rest of his natural life. And the call for him to be impeached in Parliament on a charge linking treason with Impersonating a Chief Operating Officer seemed way over the top to me. That's why I sent him a letter. Nothing special. Just a note saying I thought he was getting a raw deal.

But you could have knocked me down with a feather when the Prime Minister made his historic announcement to the nation. I'd *never* expected that Pratt's dad would simply be given his job back.

True, as the PM said, previous records count for nothing when it comes to managing England. And yes, Pratt's dad could hardly make a bigger mess of it than most of his predecessors. But still I had these nagging doubts. Didn't you need *some* inside knowledge of football to run a national team? Being positive in the face of adversity was all very well. And Ron Pratt had that in spades. But didn't you need to prepare players for penalty shootouts? Didn't you have to know how to make tactical substitutions?

Q: CAN YOU NAME THE TWO CURRENT MANCHESTER UNITED STARS WHO ARE AMONG ONLY SIX PLAYERS EVER TO BE SENT OFF WHILE PLAYING FOR ENGLAND?

Over the next couple of weeks, everywhere you went people were debating who might be in Pratt's dad's first squad. On Day One he had promised a "brand new look" to the team, and warned that he had "a few fresh ideas" that he wanted to "put into place". He didn't exactly have the easiest fixture to kick off with. Germany are tough opponents at any time. And in this vital World Cup qualifier they certainly weren't going to take any prisoners. I suppose I should have been shocked when Pratt the Younger was then appointed to be his dad's "Technical Director". But by that stage I was well into Shock Overkill. If Ron Pratt could manage England with no background whatsoever in football, why shouldn't a kid with a neat bike and a face like Kate Winslet be his Number Two?

Even so, I wasn't expecting to get my last phone call from him.

"Long time, no see," the new Technical Director said, and we chewed the fat for a while. He seemed keen to know how I was getting on at school and everything. When I told him I'd switched from Sciences to Music, Art and Drama for my A levels, he said that sounded like a good move. I didn't mention, at the time, that I was just as bad at the new stuff as I was at the old. I didn't want to sound like a *complete* failure in comparison to him.

"So how about you?" I said in the end, wondering when he was going to offer me tickets for the Germany game. "You've landed on your feet, haven't you?"

"It's good of you to say so, Jermaine," he replied. "But my dad's right: attitude counts for so much. You get what you deserve in this life. Nothing more, nothing less. Which is, of course, why you've come into the picture now."

Q: WHICH EUROPEAN CLUB WERE THE FIRST TO INTRODUCE THE CONCEPT OF TOTAL FOOTBALL?

"*Me?*" I sort of choked on the word and I don't think he heard how gobsmacked I was.

"So anyway," he went on, "you will be free for the five days leading up to Saturday, won't you?"

"*Me?*" I gasped again. "I don't know. Why?"

"You're being called up, Jermaine. You've made the squad. Dad doesn't forget people – he thinks you've got what it takes, and so do I. Your attitude, the talent you showed on that day up at Nottingham Forest, the way you sent him that letter of support when everyone else was after his blood. We're getting all the lads together initially at Bisham Abbey. Then we'll fly out. I'm not sure at present where in Germany we touch down. Athens, perhaps? Moscow...?" He paused, I waited, then he exploded with laughter. "No, no, Jermaine, really! I'm just having a joke. I *know* those places aren't in Germany. It's Hamburg we're heading for. *Franz-Joseph-Strauss-Flughafen*. That's the airport. You do have a current passport, now don't you?"

I tried to speak but I couldn't make a sound. In fact I didn't think, then, that I would ever say another word. It didn't seem to matter to Pratt, though.

"We can't guarantee you a start in the game, Jermaine," he was saying. "Not this time around. But it'll be good for you to bed down with the squad, get to know the set-up. Dad really does believe in you. Between you and me, he's sure that your chance will come sooner rather than later. Anyway, look, I'd love to keep chatting but I've still got fifteen other guys in the squad to notify. So I'll have to say *Ciao* for now, and wait until we get to Bisham Abbey to catch up with each other properly. Oh, and Jermaine – congratulations!"

Q: WHAT NICKNAME DID THE PRESS GIVE TO SAUDI ARABIA'S SAYEED AL-OWAIRAN AFTER HIS SIXTY YARD DRIBBLE AND WINNING SHOT AGAINST BELGIUM IN THE 1994 WORLD CUP FINALS?

*   *   *

That was twelve hours ago. I haven't slept all night. Most of the time I wandered around town, waiting for the shops to open so I could buy the newspapers. And there it all was in black and white:

Pratt Puts Faith in Schoolboy Stunner!
Pratt Goes Out on a Limb for Torso!
It's Jermaine Versus Germany!
Will Torso Have the Legs for Crucial Qualifier?
There's Only One Jermy Torso!

I'm in, and that's the bottom line. When I got home, you gents of the press were already encamped on my front doorstep. And five players' agents were fighting (literally) with each other to get me to sign up with them before I spoke to you. Twelve hours is a long time in football.

I think it's fair to say that I did, in the beginning, think of withdrawing from the squad. But at the end of the day, in the grey light of dawn, I really couldn't see why I should. I mean, this is the modern world. And when you weigh it up, it *is* all about mental strength. You've got to listen to the man: attitude counts for so much. OK, I said back there that I'm not Kevin Keegan. But he wasn't Kevin Keegan either when he started out. He *made* himself Kevin Keegan.

As the boss himself once put it, I've got to see this as a challenge. There's no such thing as a job for life any more, even if you've never actually had a job in the first place. And to be absolutely honest, I've had it up to here with coming bottom in

Q: WHERE WOULD YOU FIND THE FOXES?

Art, Drama and Music. So, finally, in answer to the question that you all want to put to me: Yes, I'm *really* up for this. I agree with my new agent that destiny is calling, and I'm going to give a loud and clear answer back.

And now if you don't mind, I've got an appointment with a boot sponsor. . .

copyright: *Jermaine Torso, as dictated to Neil Veal, players' agent – Mr Torso's sole accredited representative – currently considering offers for any quality product endorsements, not necessarily connected with sport.*

Quiz Answers

Following Pompey

p97 Elton John.

p98 John Major.

p99 Swindon Town.

p100 Scotland.

p101 Denmark.

p102 Andy Cole with five strikes against Ipswich Town.

p103 Wales!

p104 Ajax.

p105 On December 26th 1935 he became the first player to score an extraordinary triple hat-trick during his side's thirteen-four win against Oldham Athletic.

p106 Dixie Dean. He netted sixty times for Everton in 1927–28.

p108 Northwich Victoria's Drill Field, built in 1874.

p109 Eusebio of Portugal.

p110 As well as a TV pundit, Jimmy is also a qualified linesman and was called to pitchside as an emergency replacement.

p111 Paris St Germain.

p112 Cameroon.

Pratt's Dad

p117 Majed Abdullah of Saudi Arabia.

p118 Marlow and Maidenhead.

p119 Uruguay.

p121 1971. Southampton beat Stewarton and Thistle.

p122 Gary Lineker.

p123 Benfica's Stadium of Light.

p124 Wolves.

p125 David Beckham and Paul Scholes.

p126 Ajax.

p127 The Desert Maradona.

p128 Leicester City.

The Shirt on Your Back

Alan Durant

For Kit,
in return for a step-over

I caught football at the age of eight. My primary school's best football player supported Manchester United, so I did too – and have done ever since. I've often thought it would have been easier had I supported a local team, but once it's in your blood that's it. Now my son is carrying on the tradition.

I've written quite a few novels, and contributed *A Christmas Carol – Second Leg* to NICE ONE, SANTA! This story was my wife's idea. Nice one, Jinny!

Mark had been waiting all day for this moment. For days and days, weeks even, he'd thought about it, imagined how it would be, anticipated it with delicious excitement – the moment when he'd unwrap his Christmas presents from Mum and Dad. And one present in particular. The one he was holding now, light and squashy, wrapped in jolly red Father Christmas paper. This was the present he'd been waiting for since he'd made out his Christmas list several weeks before.

He'd had some presents already – the small gifts from Santa that he'd found in the large sock at the end of his bed. It was the usual sort of stuff: chocolate, a notepad, a pen, a pencil and a rubber, a torch, a football game, a diary (Manchester United, of course), some bubble bath (also Man U), a "big head" football figure (David Beckham in England strip) and lots of other little things that had kept him busy for half an hour or so. But it was the presents under the Christmas tree downstairs that had been at the top of his mind almost from the instant he'd woken up. He'd had to wait for several hours though, before the moment had come to open them.

First, there was breakfast (a proper sit-down affair with grapefruit, cereal, toast and eggs, to the accompaniment of Mum's old carols disc), then there was church (why did the Christmas service always go on so?), then there was the wait while Dad collected Grandma and Grandad and settled them in with drinks and whatever else they needed... Sometimes it

Q: WHICH ENGLISH LEAGUE SIDE RECENTLY MOVED FROM ELM PARK TO THE MADEJSKI STADIUM?

seemed as if Christmas morning was a kind of endurance test set by adults, Mark thought. How *could* they make him wait so long to open his presents? Many of his friends, he knew, opened all their presents as soon as they got up – his classmate, Chris, had been riding his new bike along the street at half past seven! But in Mark's house things were different.

"It's good to wait," Mum had said when he'd asked her about it at breakfast. "It makes you appreciate the day more."

"Think yourself lucky," Dad had added. "My mum and dad made us wait till after lunch before opening our presents."

"After lunch!" Mark had cried, horrified. "That's cruel!"

"I think I agree with you," Dad had laughed. "But Mum's right, a little bit of waiting keeps the pot simmering nicely. Speaking of which, who's for another cup of tea?"

How the morning had dragged! Even Grandma and Grandad had seemed to take longer than usual to get settled. Grandad had told a long story about a fox that he'd seen on his allotment early that morning, and Grandma had a tale about the next door neighbour's cat chasing a robin around the garden. They'd been interesting enough stories and Mark would have enjoyed listening to them – after the presents had been opened! Finally, though, the moment had arrived.

He squeezed the present before starting to unwrap it, delighting in its reassuring squashiness. Then his fingers tore at the red paper, ripping the sticky tape and shredding Father Christmasses... In seconds, the gift was free of its wrapping and plain for all to see. Grandad uttered a sigh of satisfaction.

"Ooh, isn't that lovely?" cooed Grandma.

Mark, however, said nothing. He stared at the football shirt in

Q: WHICH SCOTTISH SIDE ARE KNOWN AS THE GERS?

his hands with a look of bewilderment. It wasn't red as he'd expected; it was claret with sky-blue sleeves. The grin that had been on his face an instant before quickly vanished.

"It's a Burnley shirt," he said with quiet incomprehension.

"That's right," said Dad jauntily. "Turn it round. Take a look at the back."

Mark did as he was bidden. On the back was written "Mark" just above a number seven. Mark continued to stare without expression. "I thought it was going to be a Manchester United shirt," he murmured, unable to disguise his disappointment. "I asked for a Manchester United shirt."

"You've got United's kit already," said Mum. "Dad thought you'd like a Burnley shirt. He's got you tickets for the game tomorrow, too."

"That's right," Dad beamed. "You can wear your new shirt."

Burnley were the local team. Dad had supported them since he was a boy; Grandad supported them too. Mark supported Manchester United. He'd wanted the latest Manchester United shirt with the number seven and "Beckham" on the back, like some of his friends had. He wasn't interested in Burnley.

"I've got *last year*'s Manchester United shirt," he explained almost reproachfully. "I wanted the new one." His throat had started to tighten and he could feel the tears coming. "I didn't ask for a Burnley shirt. I asked for a Manchester United one." His voice was shaky and shrill.

"Mark, you should be ashamed of yourself!" Mum chided. "Dad went to a lot of trouble getting that shirt for you."

"It's a lovely shirt," Grandma enthused once more.

"But it's the wrong one!" Mark howled and, with the tears

Q: WHAT DID PORTSMOUTH'S MANAGER JACK TINN ATTRIBUTE HIS SIDE'S FA CUP SUCCESS IN 1939 TO?

uncontainable now, he dropped the shirt and ran from the room.

Surely it wasn't asking too much for Mum and Dad to get him the shirt he'd asked for, the shirt of the team he loved, he complained to himself as he lay on his bed. It wasn't as if he'd asked for the whole kit like some kids did. All he wanted was the new shirt. He'd had his old one since last Christmas; it wasn't unreasonable for him to want to have one that was more up to date . . . was it? If Mum and Dad were going to spend money on a shirt, then why not buy him the one he wanted? Why buy him a Burnley shirt? If he'd wanted that, then he'd have put it on his list. But he didn't. Why would he? He didn't support Burnley. No one supported Burnley – only grown-ups like Dad and Grandad. None of the kids at Mark's school did. They all supported Man U. If he went out to play football with a Burnley shirt on his back, he'd be laughed off the pitch. It was all so unfair. Christmas only came once a year and now it was ruined. Everything was ruined.

Mark had been lying about in misery for a quarter of an hour or so, when Grandad appeared. Mark pouted sulkily, anticipating a lecture. But when Grandad spoke, his tone was gentle and reassuring.

"Ee, lad, you've got a face like a rainy Tuesday," he said. "How about we take a walk up the allotment, eh? Work up an appetite like." He smiled affectionately. "It's a while since we had a good natter, you and I."

It was all a set-up, Mark knew. They were trying to win him round to accepting that stupid Burnley shirt. Well, he wouldn't.

 **Q:** WHO WAS THE FIRST PLAYER TO WIN THE COVETED WORLD PLAYER OF THE YEAR AWARD?

He didn't really want to stay on his bed all Christmas, though. And it was true, he and Grandad hadn't had a chat for a while. Maybe he could get him on his side. Get him to talk to Dad.

"OK," he said.

The allotment was only up the end of the road. Mark and Grandad put on their coats and started walking. The street was empty and quiet. It was a cool, sunless day, the sky patchy with grey clouds. There was a hint of rain in the air.

They walked in silence at first, the only sound their feet tapping on the pavement. As they passed by the houses, Mark glanced at the Christmas trees in the windows. He thought of the presents that would have been under them and the pleasure they would have brought. He bet there was no one there who felt as let down and miserable as him. He bet there was no one there who'd been given a Burnley shirt when they'd asked specifically for the new Manchester United one.

"He loves Burnley you know, your dad," Grandad said at last, almost as if he could read Mark's thoughts. "Just as I do."

"I know," Mark muttered.

"He wants you to like them too," Grandad went on.

"Don't I know it," Mark grumbled.

"Yes, well," said Grandad. "I've told him before, you can't *make* someone like a team. They either like them or they don't. It's a passion." They continued walking in silence for a few moments. "Happen you're passionate about Manchester United, eh?" he asked.

"Yes," Mark nodded. "They're great. They're the best."

"Ah," Grandad uttered with a small shake of his head. He smiled. "They are the best team just now," he agreed. "Though

Q: WHO PLAY THEIR HOME GAMES AT THE MAGNIFICENT NOU CAMP?

it wasn't always so." His smile grew broader. "Burnley were top dogs once, you know."

"Yes, Dad's told me," Mark said, adding with a small rueful smile of his own, "Lots of times. They won the league the year he was born."

"Aye, that's right," Grandad confirmed. "Nineteen sixty. They beat Manchester City on the last day of the season to sneak past Wolves and win the championship. It was the first time they'd been top all season." He sighed with pleasure at the memory. "Of course, it was Wolves that were the great side in those days. If they'd won that year, they'd have had a hat-trick of titles. As it was, they had to make do with winning the cup." He nodded his head wryly. "Not such a bad consolation."

They'd reached the allotment now. The gates were shut. They were, it seemed, the only ones to visit that Christmas morning.

"That Wolves team sound like Man Utd now," Mark suggested, as Grandad fiddled with the lock.

Grandad paused for a moment and looked thoughtful. "Aye," he affirmed, "I guess you could say that." His thoughtfulness turned to amusement. "Only better, mind." He chuckled and Mark laughed too – a brief, half-dismissive laugh, but a laugh nonetheless. Grandad could always make him laugh, even when, like now, he was feeling grouchy and down in the dumps. He had this way of being able to take the heat out of any situation. Grandma often said he could charm the birds out of the trees.

Well, he could certainly charm amazing vegetables out of his allotment. It always looked in perfect condition – even on winter days like this when the world was drab and dull and everything

Q: WHO WAS THE FIRST PLAYER IN LEAGUE HISTORY TO AMASS TWO HUNDRED GOALS?

seemed to be dead or sleeping, waiting for spring, Grandad still managed to produce good things to eat.

"We'll take back a couple of cabbages," he said. "They'll go nicely with the turkey."

He went over to the potting shed where he kept his tools. Mark sat down on a large upturned pot. He watched Grandad for a bit, as he dug up the cabbages then pottered about tending his patch. As he sat, Mark thought about Dad's present. He didn't feel so bitter now, just sort of sad about what had happened. He got on very well with his dad as a rule and he was sorry that they'd had a row – and on Christmas Day too. If only he'd given him what he'd asked for...

"Your dad was really chuffed with that shirt, you know," Grandad said.

"Yes, I know," Mark murmured. "He wants me to support Burnley, but I can't. I support Man Utd." He blew out his cheeks wistfully. "I wish he'd got me tickets to see *them* play."

Grandad snorted. "It's easier to get an audience with Her Majesty the Queen than to get tickets to see United," he remarked. "Happen you'll have to wait till they play the Clarets." The Clarets was Burnley's nickname.

"But—" Mark started to protest. He was about to say that that could never happen, seeing as Burnley were down the bottom of Division Two and United were top of the Premiership, but he stopped himself just in time. He didn't want to hurt Grandad's feelings. It wasn't his fault that Dad had given him the wrong shirt.

"Next year in the cup," Grandad suggested.

"Mmm," Mark muttered, unconvinced.

Q: CAN YOU NAME THE KEEPER WHO BROKE HIS NECK DURING THE 1956 FA CUP FINAL BUT MANAGED TO PLAY ON AND HELP WIN THE TROPHY?

Grandad turned over another large pot and sat down beside Mark. He looked at his grandson with unusual earnestness. "You *will* wear that shirt to the match tomorrow, won't you, lad?" he asked.

Mark shrugged. "Mmm," he muttered again non-committally. The truth was, he didn't want to go to the match. There was a Man Utd game on TV in the afternoon and he'd been looking forward to watching that. Now he'd miss it, and for what? To see Burnley play some other struggling team. It'd probably be boring as hell. But there was no way he could get out of it, he could see that.

"Will you be coming to the match too?" he enquired hopefully.

"Aye," said Grandad. "Wild horses couldn't tear me away."

On the way home, Grandad told Mark some more stories about Burnley. Their history was one of spectacular highs and lows. They were one of the original members of the League way back in 1888 and first won the championship in 1921, when they set a record of thirty games in a row without defeat. In recent times, though, the club had struggled – in 1987 they'd almost gone out of the League. Only a win on the last day of the season had saved them.

The period Grandad liked talking about best was the sixties, when the team had been among the best in the land. "They were still in the top-flight when your dad started supporting them," Grandad told Mark. "I took him to his first game in nineteen sixty-eight. They beat Fulham two-nil. And in those days Fulham had some top players: George Cohen from the sixty-six World Cup-winning team; Johnny Haynes and Allan

Q: WHICH IS THE ONLY SCOTTISH SIDE TO HAVE LIFTED THE EUROPEAN CUP?

Clarke, who went on to play for Leeds United. Burnley weren't short of talent either. They had Ralph Coates, Andy Lochhead, Willie Morgan – he went on to captain your lot, of course."

"What, Man Utd?" Mark's interest suddenly increased ten-fold.

"Aye," Grandad confirmed. "They signed him not long after they won the European Cup. Nearly broke your dad's heart it did. Willie Morgan was his favourite player."

"Maybe that's why he doesn't like Man Utd," Mark said.

Grandad shook his head. "No, lad," he said. "It's not that he doesn't like your lot. It's more that he loves Burnley – and he finds it difficult to accept that you don't."

They were back where they started, Mark thought, appre-hension rising as they approached home. "I don't know how I'd have felt if he'd supported another team," Grandad continued. "I'm not trying to get you to change your allegiance, lad. I just want you to understand why he's done what he's done. See things from his side." Grandad put his hand on Mark's shoulder as they arrived at the front gate. "And be kind to him, eh?" he implored softly.

Mark nodded. The disappointment was still there, deep in his stomach, but the resentment had waned in the light of a growing sympathy for Dad. He wished he hadn't behaved as he had when he'd opened the present. What must Grandma have thought, he wondered uncomfortably? He must have seemed like a real spoilt brat.

Grandad appeared to sense Mark's discomfort, for he added, reassuringly, "There's no need to say owt. It's all forgotten. Let's

Q: HOW MANY TIMES HAVE BRAZIL LIFTED THE WORLD CUP?

just enjoy our Christmas, eh? I don't know about you, lad, but I'm starved."

It seemed that everything had indeed been forgotten. There was no mention of the Burnley shirt, or the match the next day, or Mark's outburst. Christmas dinner was as jolly as ever – with crackers and jokes and lots of delicious food. Grandad's vegetables, it was agreed, were a real highlight.

The rest of the day passed in equal harmony. They played games, watched TV, ate, drank, chatted, laughed... It was as if the unpleasantness of the morning had never been. Family unity and the spirit of the season prevailed.

Mark went along with the mood, but he couldn't forget what had happened. Lying in bed that night, looking at the Burnley shirt at the bottom of his bed, he felt a renewed pang of disappointment. It had been a good day, but now it was over and there wasn't much to look forward to, it seemed. For weeks he'd imagined himself playing football in his new David Beckham shirt, and now it was not to be. Tomorrow he was off to a football match, which should have been exciting. But Burnley v Chesterfield just didn't set his pulse racing somehow. It was the anticlimax to end what had already been a let-down.

On Boxing Day after lunch, however, he dutifully put on his Burnley shirt and set out for the match with Dad and Grandad. Dad had programmed the video so that they could watch the Man Utd game when they got back.

"After the high drama we're going to witness at Turf Moor, we'll need a little light entertainment," he joked. Mark just smiled pityingly.

 **Q:** HOW MANY ENGLISH PLAYERS HAVE BEEN NAMED WORLD FOOTBALLER OF THE YEAR?

His first view of the ground that match day, though, was indeed dramatic. They came to the crest of a hill and there was the stadium at the bottom, dominating the surrounding rows of terraced houses, and, with people flocking towards it, it was an impressive sight.

Inside was impressive too. There were stands on all four sides of the pitch. At one end – the "Bee Hole End" Dad called it – was the new East Stand, which seemed to be mainly for families. At the opposite end was the Endsleigh Stand, where the Chesterfield supporters were gathered. Then there was the Bob Lord Stand (named after the club's most famous chairman) and opposite that was the North Stand, where Mark and Dad and Grandad sat. That looked modern too.

"This place has changed beyond recognition over the past ten years or so," said Grandad. "It's not so long ago that you had to go all around the houses to get from one end of the ground t'other." He paused reflectively. "Of course," he added. "It was mainly standing in those days. Seats were for toffs."

Mark looked about him. There weren't any toffs that he could see. But there were, he was surprised to note, quite a few children and, many of them, like him, wore claret and sky blue shirts on their backs. He even recognized a couple of boys who went to his school. So it *wasn't* only grown-ups who supported Burnley...

As kick-off time approached, the crowd became more excited, the chanting more intense. At last the home team appeared, greeted by a huge roar and fervent applause. Instinctively, in spite of his avowed indifference, Mark found himself joining in.

Q: HOW MANY FA CUP FINALS SINCE WORLD WAR TWO HAVE GONE TO EXTRA TIME?

On either side of him, Dad and Grandad cheered lustily. Then Grandad turned and gave Mark a huge wink.

"It's going to be a good 'un this afternoon, I can feel it," he proclaimed confidently. Mark grinned in reply. He'd never seen Grandad so animated before.

As it happened, Grandad's optimism wasn't misplaced. The home team started superbly and soon took the lead, one of their central defenders rising high, unmarked, to head home a corner. As one, the Burnley crowd were on their feet, shouting with jubilation. Dad threw his hands in the air, then gave Mark a big hug. A moment later, Grandad did the same.

It wasn't long before this scene was repeated. Within minutes Burnley scored again, in almost identical circumstances to the first goal – this time a header from a free kick. Once again the scorer was unmarked. Now it was Mark who initiated the celebrations, leaping up quickly and throwing his arms around Dad, then Grandad. He'd really started to enjoy himself. He'd never imagined that coming to see Burnley play would be this much fun.

"Ee, steady on there, lad," said Grandad, taken aback by the vigour of Mark's embrace. "They haven't won yet, you know. There's a long way to go..." He looked across at Dad and shook his head – but his face wore a broad smile.

At half-time, the score was still two-nil and not even the weak tea and watery orange drink Dad bought could dilute their euphoria. They exchanged views happily about what they had seen and what was to come in the second half – more goals, they expected. After a bright start though, the home team lost their way a little. The play became scrappy and unimaginative.

Q: CAN YOU NAME THE MANAGER WHO LED ENGLAND TO VICTORY IN THE 1966 WORLD CUP FINALS?

Midway through the half, Chesterfield pulled a goal back and from then on, the game was in the balance. Both sides had chances to score and wasted them and the last minutes were as tense as anything Mark had experienced in his life. At last, the referee blew the final whistle and Mark stood and cheered with the rest of the home supporters. Mark's first Burnley match had ended in victory – just as Dad's had over thirty years before.

"We'll have to take you every week," said Grandad jovially, as they walked home. "It's weeks since they won a game."

"Perhaps they tried extra hard because it was Christmas," Mark suggested. "They wanted to give their fans a present."

Grandad nodded, enjoying the thought. "Aye, happen they did, lad," he muttered.

"We certainly deserve it," Dad commented wryly. "Mind you," he added, "I think it was the Chesterfield defence giving the presents today!"

"Yeah," Mark agreed. Walking along the street between Dad and Grandad, part of the stream of contented fans in claret and sky blue, he felt a sudden rush of happiness. The atmosphere of good cheer was so strong he felt as if he could grasp hold of it.

Back home, Mark, Dad and Grandad chatted about the game with Mum and Grandma, reliving the highlights.

It wasn't until after tea and Christmas cake that they settled down to watch the videoed Manchester United match. In his preoccupation with the Burnley game, Mark had almost forgotten about it. Now, though, he was all excitement once more. It was an important match – but then wasn't every Man Utd game?

 Q: WHO IS ARGENTINA'S ALL-TIME TOP GOALSCORER?

"Aren't you going to put your Man Utd shirt on, then?" Dad prompted, as the teams appeared on the screen.

Mark looked down at his new Burnley shirt, then shook his head. "Nah," he said. "I'm happy wearing this." His eyes moved from the shirt to Dad. "Thanks for giving it to me, Dad," he said. "And thanks for taking me to the game." He gave Dad and Grandad a warm smile. "I like Burnley," he said. Then, after a brief pause, added, "They're my *second* best team."

Dynamite Dave

Benson Maborosi

To PJS . . .
and Chalky White's knees

Benson Maborosi was born in Omagari, Japan. It's thousands of miles from Old Trafford, so he should have supported Man U. Instead, he was seduced by rare footage of Colin Duncan scoring for the Royals – he's followed them ever since.

Benson's other passion is motor racing. He currently drives for Team Tudhope and hopes to follow in the footsteps of F1 heroes Katayama and Takagi, but with faster boots.

"**B**umper crowd tonight, innit," Linvoy Pope snorted as he entered the changing room. "Two little kids and a man with his flippin' dog!"

Kev looked up from scraping last-week's mud off his boots. "Sounds like a record attendance," he grinned.

Ataru Moroboshi, the Franburn Falcons' nippy little left-winger, peered through a grimy window. "It's early doors yet," he said, turning to face the others. "Why did Mr Badfinger want us here so soon, anyway?"

They shrugged. Franburn's head had sent a message round that afternoon: the under-fourteens were to be at the ground a full fifty minutes before kick-off.

"He's probably gonna suspend us if we lose this one," grunted Malcolm "Long Arm" Wilson, the team's spidery-limbed keeper.

The others looked grim. Their season had been dogged by injuries and bad luck. But for the tactical wizardry of coach, Billy Tudster, they'd have been bottom of the league well before Christmas. As it was, defeat against the Adbury Arrows tonight would see them relegated for the first time in the school's history.

"Ah, come on," said Linvoy chirpily, trying to lift the others. "We can do the Arrows, no probs. Their defence is almost as leaky as ours."

Ataru threw a damp sock at him. "Yeah, but we haven't exactly been piling the goals in, have we, *Shearer*!"

Q: WHICH PREMIERSHIP SIDE ARE NICKNAMED THE VILLANS?

The big striker's snappy come-back was drowned by his team-mates' jeers, then they too were lost beneath some impressively loud throat-clearing.

"Glad to see you're all in such high spirits," Mr Badfinger smiled, bustling into the centre of the room. "But settle down for a minute and give me some hush."

The boys gathered round, casting nervous glances at one another.

As usual, the head came straight to the point. "Mr Tudster's not well," he announced, long-faced. "He won't be coming."

The boys gasped. Franklin, Linvoy's partner up front, sat down with a bump. "What's happened, sir?" he asked in a small voice.

Mr Badfinger shook his head sadly. "Bit of a freak accident really. Some sort of allergic reaction to Welkers Crisps... His face is blown up like a beachball."

Everyone groaned. This was a *disaster*! How could they hope to beat the Arrows without their coach's wise words?

"Boys, boys!" Mr Badfinger protested. "It's not all bad. Far from it." He paused, and grinned briefly. "In fact, it could turn out rather well for us."

John Davies, the side's bullet-headed centre-back, pulled a face. "With respect, sir. *How?* It's nearly kick-off time. We don't have a manager. We haven't discussed tactics. We don't know *anything* about the opposition, and we're *About To Be Relegated*!" He stopped, red-cheeked and panting. The head put a calming hand on his shoulder.

"I know it's a shock – especially before such a crucial match. But don't worry. I've been speaking to an old contact, back from

Q: WHICH MULLETT-HAIRED INTERNATIONAL GOALIE IS FAMED FOR HIS SPECTACULAR "SCORPION KICK"?

my playing days, and I've pulled off quite a coup. A real fillip for Franburn School. You've got a new manager, boys – for one game only. A very *special* manager. And he's here to meet you now."

Linvoy groaned and clapped his hand over his eyes. Mr Badfinger was forever talking in assembly about how he'd "once been a professional footballer". As if second division City were a *proper* team! What old fossil had he dug up to coach them? Some retired groundsman? A former boot-boy? A knackered old team-mate—

The door to the changing-room banged open.

In walked an *extremely* familiar figure, dressed in a razor-sharp Armani suit, sleeves rolled up to the elbows, and wearing a *very* famous TV-friendly grin.

There was a thud. Linvoy hit the floor in a dead faint.

The squad were squeezed on to the rickety bench in an awe-struck line.

Dave Dagenham! *"Dynamite"* Dave Dagenham! Relegation escapologist supreme! He'd kept Rovers up for five years on a shoe-string budget. He'd fought off the drop at Palace right through the eighties. He'd even saved United from the unthinkable... He was a living legend – and he was in their dressing room!

Of course, he'd been out of management for a while now, but *everyone* still recognized him – it was hard not to. If he wasn't giving expert summaries for The Big Match or Radio Five Live, he was opening some massive footballing mega-store or advertising some cutting-edge sporting product. A

Q: WHICH LARGER-THAN-LIFE SOCCER MANAGER AND TV PUNDIT COINED THE PHRASES "EARLY DOORS" AND "THE UGLY BALL"?

sporting product not unlike the one he held in his hands right now.

"This, lads, is rev-o-lutionary. State-of-the-art. Made to my own cunning design. I had a load knocked up as soon as 'The Finger' called me." Dynamite turned the football shirt slowly in his hands for all the players to see. Bulbous gold and onyx rings flashed as he stroked the bright material with loving fingers. "All the top clubs will be using 'em soon. Special lightweight design, see. Breathable fabric too."

He dipped into a large box and pulled out an armful, tossing one to each amazed player. "You wouldn't believe how much energy you lose wearing them old-style kits. These – and the matching micro-shorts – will give you an extra yard on them Arrows boys – guaranteed." He paused, and his left eye-lid twitched slightly. "At least, they *will* be guaranteed, once the lab results are in…" He harrumphed noisily, stepping back while the squad eagerly shed their clothes.

Only Kev hesitated, eyeing the tiny white micro-shorts warily. They were so … *micro*. The shirt was dubiously bright too… Then he shrugged. Everyone else seemed to like the kit. Quickly he wriggled into the shorts and plunged his head through the top.

"Right!" Dynamite boomed, eyes sparkling. "Now you *look* the part, let's talk *tactics*."

The team settled back on the bench. This ought to be good, thought Franklin. He looked around expectantly for a white-board and its accompanying brightly-coloured markers. He was to be disappointed.

"First of all. I don't believe in all this modern statistical nonsense. Hard graft and common sense – that's what wins

Q: IN WHICH CITY WOULD YOU FIND BOTH BRAMALL LANE AND HILLSBOROUGH?

matches." Dynamite glared at the boys, daring them to disagree. Franklin dropped his eyes to the floor guiltily. The others folded their arms; pie-eyed attentive.

The coach nodded approvingly. "We'll get on well together," he murmured, drawing a fat cigar from his top pocket and lighting it carefully. After a long drag, he unveiled his plan:

"Three across the back. Six in midfield. That's how we'll play it. We can drop the big lad –" he pointed at Linvoy – "into the centre of the park, and you –" he gestured next at Duncan, John's partner in the heart of defence – "can shift up from the back."

The boys looked at each other. That sounded a bit … basic. Somehow they'd expected something a little more insightful.

"Er… We do have to *win* this, Mr Dagenham," Ataru pointed out. "A draw won't do us any good. Shouldn't we be a little bit more … um … attack-minded?"

Dynamite waved a bejewelled hand dismissively. "The whole idea is to *stifle* their attacking players, *then* catch 'em on the break," he explained in a slow and over-patient tone. "It's worked for me in many a relegation dog-fight."

Several players nodded vigorously. If it was good enough for the Premier League, it was good enough for them.

Ataru scowled into the floor. He hated being patronized, and this strategy sounded well dodgy to *him*. He started to open his mouth again, then thought better of it. The others seemed captivated by the charismatic coach.

What little coaching he did.

Apparently the team-talk was already over. Dynamite was dragging a second hefty box across the changing room. From it

Q: WHO WON THE GOLDEN BOOT AWARD AT THE 1998 WORLD CUP FINALS?

he drew a bright-red canister bearing the slogan: "I could do with a DD!"

"You've probably seen this on the telly, lads," he panted, unscrewing the thick plastic lid. "Me own patented Double Dynamite drink. It knocks spots off that cheapo isotonic stuff – helps you run all night!" He took a swig and sighed happily. "Get 'em down your necks. Then start kicking in. I've got a press conference to attend!"

"A press conference!" Ataru hissed, the moment the changing-room door slammed. "Who does he think he's managing here?"

"He's right, though," Kev reported, nose pressed to the grubby window. "There's three newspaper guys out there, *and* a TV crew!"

"Cool!" yelled Duncan, pushing past to have a butchers himself. "We're gonna be famous!"

Ataru snorted. "You reckon? With *these* tactics? We'll be lucky if we can beat a drum."

Long Arm looked up thoughtfully from rummaging in the drinks box. "I dunno. We could do with playing more defensive. Your kamikaze breaks have cost us a heap of goals already this year." He tossed canisters to John and Kev, then rooted for some more. "We *definitely* can't afford to concede any today. Besides. He is Dynamite Dave, remember."

Ataru scowled again. "What do you reckon, Linvs?" he asked, turning to the big striker. Linvoy gazed up, rubbing his head. "Wha'?"

"Oh, never mind." The winger muttered, grabbing his boots and jamming them on.

 **Q:** WHO WAS THE FIRST EVER EUROPEAN FOOTBALLER OF THE YEAR?

"Chill out," Duncan said, hopping down from the bench and shimmying past an imaginary opponent. "Dynamite's a top manager, there's TV here to see us win and we've got an ace new kit for free. What can possibly go— Hey!" He spun round, pawing at his suddenly sodden back, glaring at Long Arm who was doubled over, coughing and spitting. "What did you do that for?"

"Sorry, man," the keeper wheezed, gasping for breath. "It's this Double Dynamite stuff. It's Double Disgusting!"

The others sniffed at their drinks suspiciously. Franklin took a small sip and gagged. Rushing across the room, he gobbed the foul pink liquid into the wall-sink, emptying the remainder of the canister quickly after it. The rest of the squad queued up to follow suit.

Except for John. He was still swigging greedily when the ref called them out to the pitch.

The Arrows looked extremely nervous when they spotted the Falcons' new coach on the touchline. And they became even more concerned when they saw how fired up the Falcons were.

Franklin was bouncing from foot to foot in the centre-circle. Long Arm was catching everything John punted at him in the box. Even Kev looked focused: making practice sprints down the byline – although he twice pulled up short, fiddling with his waistband and frowning.

There was no doubt about it: the Falcons oozed confidence.

For about five seconds.

As the Arrows kicked off, it suddenly dawned on the home players that they had no idea who was supposed to be playing

Q: WHO ARE THE ONLY MAJOR EUROPEAN LEAGUE SIDE WHO REFUSE TO HAVE A SHIRT SPONSOR?

where – let alone who they should mark. Several looked towards the bench for guidance, but Dynamite wasn't watching the action. Instead, he was deep in conversation with an immaculately-dressed elderly gentleman, over by the car park. The boys milled about in panic.

Adbury couldn't believe their luck. Within moments they had Long Arm diving at full stretch to finger a fierce shot round the post. And, from the resultant corner, they almost scrambled a goal. The ball bobbling dangerously about the box until John made a lucky connection to hack it clear. His team-mates exhaled loudly in relief.

The defender grinned and turned to Long Arm, who was scraping grass and muck from his elbow. "I reckon there's something good in that Double Dynamite. I feel *well* focused."

"You're gonna need to be," Long Arm grunted. "Here they come again!"

This time the Arrows attacked down the left flank. Their number eleven easily shook off Ataru's half-hearted challenge, setting off gleefully for the byline.

It was then that Linvoy lunged in – a makeshift midfielder delivering the classic forward's tackle: arms flailing, high leading leg, studs raised.

The startled winger travelled a short distance – straight up in the air. The ball barely moved.

The ref sprinted over, fumbling in his pocket. "That was an absolutely diabolical challenge!" he raged.

"Sorry, sir," Linvoy answered sheepishly, rubbing at his muzzy head. "I'm not used to playing back here."

Q: WHICH FORMER ENGLAND MANAGER FAMOUSLY COMPLAINED "DO I NOT LIKE THAT!"?

The ref licked the tip of his pencil, frowning. "That's no excuse, laddie. You're lucky I don't— Oi! *You!* What the heck are you playing at?"

Everyone turned to look.

Several yards away, Kev froze – bent half-over and with his shorts round his knees – his face the same beetroot red as his clearly visible pants. Several Arrows players turned swiftly away, hiding broad grins.

Kev quickly hoicked up the offending shorts, but already the man in black was barrelling over. "Bah— Bah— Bah—!" he stuttered, his own face colouring as he pointed a shaky finger at the blushing boy.

"Sorry, sir," Kev started. "I wasn't moonin' you, honest. It's these flippin' shorts. They're so itchy." He peeled back the waistband. "Look at the rash they've given me!"

The ref turned his head away, raising an arm to cover his eyes. With his free hand he swiftly brandished a card.

It was red!

"Aw, c'mon," the midfielder protested, "I've just told you—"

The ref's brows came together and he glared fiercely down his rigid arm at the Franburn boy. "*No one* makes a mockery of my authority. That was obscene gesturing, plain and simple. Now turn around and get off my pitch *right now* – and keep your shorts *on* this time!"

Furious, Kev spun on his heel and headed for touch. Satisfied, the ref at last signalled for the free kick.

Again there was pandemonium in the Falcons' ranks. Long Arm yelled for a wall and almost everyone rushed to oblige. Too late.

Q: WHO WAS THE FIRST PLAYER TO SCORE IN THREE CONSECUTIVE EUROPEAN CHAMPIONSHIP TOURNAMENTS?

The Arrows' number eight had already teed up the ball. With barely any run-up, he screamed it past the Franburn players, over Long Arm's head and into the top right-hand corner. One-nil! And one step nearer relegation!

As the scorer wheeled away and a downcast Long Arm fished the ball from the net, John gestured frantically to Duncan.

"Mate! Mate! You've gotta help me out!" He was bent almost double, one leg crossed firmly in front of the other.

Duncan looked at him in concern. "What's up? You get a knock?"

John shook his head. "No. It's that Double Dynamite. It's gone right through me. I *have* to get to the loo!"

Duncan shook his head. "I'm not surprised, the way you were necking it." He glanced up at the ref, who was busy with his notebook on the halfway line. "Go on then," he grunted, "I'll cover for you. But be *quick*!"

John scuttled off just as the whistle sounded for the restart. The Falcons soon lost possession again, but the Arrows couldn't make any momentum going forward. The ball ended up with their keeper. "Yeah, and you just keep hold of it, mate," Duncan muttered, then shot a glance at the the changing rooms. "C'mon John. Get a flippin' move on!"

The keeper launched the ball skywards.

Aided by the wind, it dropped well inside the Falcons' half – right on to the boot of the Arrows' pacy number nine. There was no way Duncan could cover the space. He raced forward but the striker rounded him effortlessly.

Long Arm dashed out and tried to make himself big. It was a futile effort. The forward had a boot like a traction engine, and

Q: HOW MANY TIMES HAVE LIVERPOOL WON THE PREMIER LEAGUE?

his shot was a ballistic missile, low and hard past the keeper's left hand. Two-nil!

The cheers from the Arrows boys brought Dynamite racing to pitch-side at last.

"Come on, lads!" he yelled, shaking a meaty fist. "You can easily pull level."

The players looked at him with a mixture of anguish and dismay. Kev stalked past dumping an armful of under-sized kit at the coach's feet. "We're *two* down, *Boss*!" he grunted.

Dynamite blanched. He could see the TV crew out of the corner of one twitching eye. Squaring his shoulders he roared out at the players: "Come on, team! Where's your shape? Where's your commitment? Remember what I told you! Work! Work! Work!"

John slunk past him, back on to the pitch. "Sorry," he whispered to Duncan.

The acting midfielder shook his head. "Weren't your fault. If it wasn't for his stupid drinks *and* his stupid kit, it'd be a different game."

With a two goal cushion, the Arrows eased off the gas. At last the Falcons could regroup. Almost unconsciously they drifted into their more familiar positions and, despite Dynamite's cries of despair, it was this that almost brought them a goal on the stroke of half-time.

Duncan found Ataru, who picked out Linvoy. His head clear at last, the striker skillfully nudged the ball into the path of his partner – only to see Franklin scuff a weak shot straight at the keeper.

 **Q:** WHO IS THE PREMIERSHIP'S ONLY KNIGHTED MANAGER?

Linvoy closed his eyes despairingly. If they missed any more chances like *that*, they'd definitely be down.

The ref had seen enough too. He blew his whistle.

As the Falcons trudged gloomily off, they heard Dynamite talking for the cameras. "I'll shake 'em up for the second half, don't you worry. *Then* they'll stick to my game-plan."

"What in Pelé's name are you playing at?" he roared, two minutes later. "Are you trying to ruin me?" He swung open the changing-room door and pointed towards the touchline. "See that old guy in the suit? That's Jack Runner – the chairman of 'Boro. He's here to offer me a mega-bucks contract. *If* you lot can just win this flippin' match!"

The boys looked at each other. "I thought you were here to help *us*..." Duncan murmured.

Dynamite laughed harshly. "Get real! There's a lot more riding on this than a stupid *schools'* match. Why do you think all them telly people are here? You lot are my ticket back to the big-time. So pull your flippin' fingers out!"

To emphasize this point he lifted his untouched teacup and hurled it forcefully at the wall.

Outside, the press pack and the very tiny crowd looked up in surprise as a terrifying yell rose from the dressing room.

Inside, Duncan hobbled for the cold shower, the remnants of a cupful of scalding tea still dripping from his lap.

The Franburn Ten were grim-faced as they jogged out for the second half. Dynamite followed, making a beeline for the TV boys. "Now we'll see," he announced smugly.

Q: WHO IS THE ONLY MAN TO HAVE APPEARED IN THREE WORLD CUP WINNING SIDES?

"What wise words did you offer the team?" the reporter queried.

Dagenham grinned, looking slyly towards Mr Runner, who was pretending not to listen. "Just gave 'em some of the good old dynamite!"

Ataru frowned at that and beckoned the others into a huddle near the centre-spot.

"The guy's a flippin' nutter," he whispered. "We were just getting it together near half-time and now he wants us to play even deeper than before!"

Duncan winced. "He must be insane. I can barely walk since he crocked me. There's no way we can deal with any more pressure at the back."

Linvoy nodded, scratching at a newly-formed blotch under his waistband. "I say we go back to our old formation. If we don't get forward we'll be relegated for sure!"

"Right." Ataru declared, glancing up at the impatient ref. "We ignore that Dagenham and play the way we know."

There was swift agreement and, high-fiving and back-slapping, they retreated to their positions.

On the touchline the newsmen looked impressed. "You certainly seem to have them motivated, Mr Dagenham."

Dynamite Dave nodded, casting another smug glance at Mr Runner and brushing an imaginary speck of lint from his suit jacket. "It's a gift," he grinned as the whistle blew.

The Falcons steamed in at once, all guns blazing.

Linvoy saw a fine shot clatter off the bar, Franklin had a powerful diving header cleared from the line and Ataru's delicious volley was spectacularly tipped round a post. The Arrows reeled.

 **Q:** WHICH FAMOUS OLD CLUB MAKE THEIR HOME AT TURF MOOR?

But with each flowing move, Dynamite became angrier and angrier. "Get back! Get back!" he roared, turning blue and gesticulating wildly. "Remember the plan!"

For some reason, none of the players seemed to hear.

He turned slowly purple.

A pressman leant forwards. "Why are you so worried? It's been all Franburn this half."

The coach took his eye off the game long enough to glare at the man. "The little idiots'll concede a hatful playing this way. If they don't keep it tight they'll ruin every— Ah..."

Out on the pitch, the home players were mobbing Linvoy. The pressure had told at last. A grass-scudding toe-poke had put them back in the match.

Dynamite opened and shut his mouth several times. No sound emerged. Jack Runner strolled over, rubbing his hands and smiling broadly. "You appear to be working your magic, Mr Dagenham," he observed.

Dynamite managed a sickly smile, then turned back towards the game. "Oi!" he hollered, waving towards Linvoy as the striker jogged back for the restart. "Drop deeper, lad. You got lucky there, but we can't afford to be cavalier!"

Linvoy nodded, gave a thumbs up and, when the ref blew his whistle, trotted off in completely the opposite direction.

"Gaaah!" Dynamite fumed. "What is the *matter* with you? Can't *any* of you follow *simple* instruct—"

Franklin stole the ball and drilled it wide to Ataru. The little winger crossed first time. Linvoy raced in unchallenged and powered home his second strike in a minute!

Q: WHICH PLAYER WON THE UNIQUE TREBLE OF WORLD PLAYER OF THE YEAR, EUROPEAN PLAYER OF THE YEAR AND AFRICAN PLAYER OF THE YEAR ALL IN 1995?

Dynamite turned white. Then extremely red. "Gaaah…
Ahh… Ha-ha!" he spluttered, acutely aware of the cameras and
Mr Runner's eyes upon him. "Good show, lads!" he blustered.
"More of the same now. Just like we … er … practised."

Franklin and Linvoy gaped at *that*. Then Ataru came running
across to high-five the goal-machine. "Can you believe his
cheek," he hissed.

Linvoy shrugged. "We've well sussed him," he whispered.
"Now let's bag that third goal, and really shut him up!"

"Linvoy! Linvoy!" Twenty minutes later the Falcons were
staggering off the pitch, their hat-trick hero held aloft.

He'd snared the winner in the final minute. Another header
from an Ataru cross. The comeback was complete! The Falcons
had escaped the drop!

John descended upon the man with the dog and gave both a
big kiss. Franklin was hugging everyone. Long Arm and Duncan
began an impromptu Irish jig on the touchline – till Kev
barrelled into them and all three fell in a laughing heap at the
feet of … Jack Runner and Dynamite Dave!

Runner had his arm around the big boss-man's shoulder. He
stepped over the boys disdainfully, guiding Dynamite towards
his car "… just the man for the job. Amazing display!" he was
enthusing to the cameraman walking alongside.

Dynamite clutched a new contract to his proudly thrust-out
chest. He didn't even glance at the Franburn boys.

For a moment their celebrations died.

"What do you think Dynamite will bring to the 'Boro, Mr
Runner?" the cameraman asked.

Q: WHO WON THE FIRST ENGLISH PLAYERS' PLAYER OF
THE YEAR AWARD IN 1974?

Jack Runner, bending to unlock the door of his car, paused. "Well, it's obvious, isn't it. He'll be working with pros again. And just think what he can achieve with them if he can totally transform a team of –" he looked down his nose at the Falcons – "no-hoper kids."

The cameraman raised an eyebrow and swivelled his equipment to catch the boys on film. "Harsh words, lads," he murmured. "Do you agree?"

Duncan snorted. John clamped a hand across his mouth. Linvoy and Kev seemed to be turning blue – they couldn't get a word out. Long Arm spoke for them all. "Oh yeah," he grinned, spreading his gangly arms wide. "He's *just right* for the Premiership. We reckon he's Double Dynamite!"

And with that, the Falcons' first eleven creased up and mobbed each other once more.

The End of the Road

Malcolm Rose

For all centre-backs in youth teams

Malcolm was never much good at football. He even supports Coventry City. The football that creeps into many of his novels like *Flying Upside Down*, *Tunnel Vision* and *Concrete Evidence*, comes from watching his son playing in a local league and through his vast experience as a linesman.

Being a linesman, he has learned many new and useful football terms from players with much better eyesight than his own.

The picture focused on the distant point where the dual carriageway narrowed to a single strip of tarmac. In the background, the sea and sky blurred into each other. Slowly, the image on the screen came closer to the football pitch where the local TV station had set up the video camera. It panned past the ancient copse, where the protestors' tree-houses looked like sturdy but untidy crows' nests among the stark branches, past the stream and finally on to the pitch itself and the TV presenter.

Sitting on the settee in front of the television, Max and his dad both shouted at the same time, "It's on!"

At once they were joined by Max's mum and Scrag the dog.

Standing in the field next to the road, the presenter was saying, "That wood behind me is soon to be cleared for the latest – and most controversial – extension of the dual carriageway. This football pitch will also be devoured by the widened road. I have with me Max Deakin, captain of Heswall Panthers Under-fifteens' team, David Fish, Highway Manager of Wirral Borough Council, and a protestor known as Earth Prince – a spokesman for the environmental group that's occupying the wood. First let me ask Max what he thinks of the last stage of this traffic development."

The microphone thrust into his face, Max said, "They're going to put it right through our field. It's not fair. If we don't have a home ground we'll get booted out the league. There's plenty of roads but this is our only pitch."

Q: WHO WAS THE FIRST BLACK PLAYER TO CAPTAIN ENGLAND?

Turning to the council officer, the interviewer said, "It doesn't sound very fair, does it, Mr Fish? The festive season's nearly here and you're playing Scrooge rather than Father Christmas to these lads."

Mr Fish grimaced. "I'm afraid we can't allow one football pitch – and a small wood – to bring traffic to a complete standstill. We've been looking into Heswall Panthers' case for some time now but, as you know, the number of pitches at our disposal are very limited. We have every sympathy with Max and his team-mates but unfortunately we've not been able to find them alternative accommodation – at least not to the standard required by their league."

"Can they share a pitch with another club?"

"Our grounds are already being shared to capacity. You see, Max may say there are lots of roads and only one football pitch for them, but actually there are lots of football clubs – too many for an area of this size. The players can always join one of the other teams."

Butting in, Earth Prince muttered, "Drivers can always use another form of transport."

"OK. Turning to you, Earth Prince. You have your own reasons for opposing this road widening."

"Yes," he replied. "Plenty. We're protecting this historic copse from being flattened by bulldozers because, as Max said, we're already suffocating with new roads. The birches and ash were here around one hundred and fifty years ago when steam-powered boats began to bring industry to Merseyside. The oaks started life at the same time as Jane Austen."

 **Q: WHAT IS SCUNTHORPE UNITED'S STEELY NICKNAME?**

Impatiently cutting him off, the interviewer asked, "Is any of this wildlife threatened?"

"It's all threatened by Mr Fish's extra lanes. But if you mean, is any of it endangered or protected by the law, as far as we know, it isn't. Yet Mr Fish plans to replace this beautiful, natural habitat with concrete and tarmac for no gain whatsoever."

"Surely drivers'll gain from the reduction in traffic chaos."

Earth Prince laughed cynically. "No they won't. You see, this is stage five of the road improvement. So, if the scheme's working, stages one to four should've helped already. But they haven't. You ask any local resident – traffic congestion's as bad as ever. The road widening's not working, so why carry on with it?"

David Fish smiled as if at a well-meaning child who'd got everything hopelessly wrong. "That's not the case. We didn't expect an improvement until *all* stages had been completed. Improving one bit of the road simply creates a bottleneck further along. We'll only get the real benefit when they're all done."

Earth Prince was not yet into his twenties but he was an experienced eco-warrior and traveller. He was a veteran of the campaign against the Newbury bypass. "And when you've completed stage five, where will the new bottleneck be? Wherever it appears, you'll have to make more so-called improvements. Where will it all end? Better roads simply make more traffic, not less traffic jams. You should be looking at alternatives to the car. You need to put your money into public transport and let Max and his team-mates carry on playing."

The interviewer brought the debate to an abrupt halt. "OK, I'll let the last word go to Max."

Q: HOW LONG DID IT TAKE PAT KRUSE OF TORQUAY TO SCORE THE QUICKEST OWN GOAL IN ENGLISH LEAGUE HISTORY?

Max's eyes fixed on David Fish and he said, "When we're a bit older, none of us'll vote for *him*."

In the Deakins' house, they all let out a cheer. "That's great," Max's mum said.

"You really laid into him," his dad added. "Well done."

Mrs Deakin said, "Let's check the video and make sure we got it on tape."

It wasn't a great pitch. On sandstone the grass always got a bit thin after a few games, but the ground was more-or-less flat. It had a rickety wooden pavilion with a separate room for the referee, it satisfied the league's requirements and it was theirs. If they lost it, they lost their membership of the local league.

The Panthers had started the season pretty well but, in the last few weeks, they'd begun to slide down the division. Max did not have to be told why. They still had the same players with the same skills, but something *was* missing.

As Max sprinted to intercept a pass that was destined for a breaking striker, he heard an unfamiliar shout from behind. "Go on, Max. That's yours!"

After he'd cleared the ball, he turned to see Earth Prince on the touchline nearest to the copse. The eco-warrior must have jumped over the sandy stream to watch the game. He was seriously weird. Unshaven, he looked like he hadn't had a bath in weeks. And his hair. There was very little of it at the sides of his head but, on top, it was dyed orange and green. He had a ring through one side of his nose and four more through his right ear. Still, he was about the only touchline supporter apart from Max's mum and Scrag. Max couldn't really count his dad who was

Q: WHICH CLUB PLAYS HOME MATCHES AT THE HAWTHORNS?

linesman, and Cameron Carter's dad who was coach and manager. Max had to admit that any shout from a supporter would be unfamiliar.

Near the end of the game, the Panthers did not even let out a groan when a shot from one of their forwards hit the post and another striker hoofed the rebound well over the bar. The team seemed resigned to defeat. Only Earth Prince let out a frustrated, "Ooo!" Then he clapped and shouted, "Nice try!"

After the three-one defeat to the mid-table side, Max noticed that Earth Prince had gone. He must have returned to his fellow travellers in the encampment. As always, Scrag was let off the lead to charge round the edges of the pitch and scrabble among the fallen leaves beside the brook. "Come away, Scrag," Mrs Deakin shouted. "It's a bit whiffy down there." Really, she didn't want him wandering across the stream and into the protestors' blockade. While Max's parents didn't like the idea of the new road, they liked the travellers even less.

Cameron, the Panthers' leading goalscorer, glanced towards the camp and said gloomily to Max, "Maybe we should concrete ourselves on to the pitch so the road people can't shift us either."

"Wouldn't present the opposition with much of a challenge, would it?" Max replied. "I can just imagine your dad yelling, 'Let's see some movement, reds. You're just standing still!'"

The lads organized their own practice session on the next Saturday because Cameron's dad was stuffed with cold. Max's dad took over as manager for the match on Sunday. That meant the Panthers were short of a linesman. They were going to have to ask the other team to supply one when Earth Prince trudged

Q: HOW MANY OF THE THREE CUP FINALS MIDDLESBOROUGH HAVE REACHED UNDER MANAGER BRYAN ROBSON DID THEY GO ON TO WIN?

towards the pitch with two other eco-warriors. "I'll do it," he volunteered.

Frowning, the ref looked him up and down then muttered, "Do you know the rules?"

Earth Prince replied with a smile, "Liverpool youth team, five years ago, before the environment took over."

"Liverpool." The ref handed over the flag. "OK. You're on."

Of course, coaching from the line wasn't allowed, but most linesmen sometimes waved the last defender forward at just the right time to catch an attacker offside. In his enthusiasm, Earth Prince did the same. He had the knack of knowing exactly when the defenders should fall back and when they should move out but he was also absolutely fair when he raised his flag. The other two travellers, just as weird as Earth Prince, shouted encouragement. They were joined in the second half by a fourth protestor, a young boy. The Panthers almost had a crowd for once. And they got a draw.

Afterwards, while Scrag made the rotting leaves fly yet again, Max went up to Earth Prince to thank him. Max didn't have a choice because no one else would. His mum and dad wouldn't go near the traveller. So it was down to the captain. He took Cameron with him for safety. "What do we call you?" asked Max. "We can't say Earth and you don't look like a prince."

The traveller laughed. "I suppose not. You can call me Adrian if you promise not to tell the police or the bailiffs. It's my real name." He introduced his friends as Birch Daughter, Holly Green and Major Survival.

 **Q:** WHO WERE THE FIRST CLUB IN FOOTBALL LEAGUE HISTORY TO CONCEDE SEVEN GOALS TO DIFFERENT PLAYERS IN ONE MATCH?

"More code-names?" Cameron asked.

One of the young women said, "No. Holly Green's my real name."

Earth Prince switched the subject back to football. "You know, you don't have much of a problem really. You're a good side. It's just that you're lacking a bit of fighting spirit, a bit of up-and-at-'em. That's all."

"We know that," Max replied.

Cameron explained, "It's only halfway through the season but the problem is, we've only got two games left before we're out the league coz we won't have a pitch. Why bother really going for it?"

Birch Daughter answered, "Because you don't give in to bullies. And you don't want to let your supporters down."

When Max heard his mum shout "Come away!" he assumed that she was calling Scrag who'd have his nose somewhere unpleasant. But she wasn't. She was yelling at Max. Embarrassed, Max said to the travellers, "Got to go."

They nodded at him and Earth Prince said, "It's OK. We understand."

Max guessed that Adrian was referring to his mum's attitude.

After being beaten away at West Kirby, the Panthers prepared for their last match before Christmas, their last home match before the bailiffs and builders moved in, their last match ever. It was against the league leaders and team morale was so low it was out of sight. At the far end of the pitch, two lorries, a van and a bulldozer had been parked. The ominous vehicles looked like a waiting enemy, eager to begin its heartless task. Within ten

Q: WHICH FOOTBALL-BASED GAME WAS REJECTED AS AN OLYMPIC SPORT IN 1992?

minutes the soulless Panthers were two goals down to Leasowe Youth.

It was then that something remarkable happened. Earth Prince came out of the copse first, like the Pied Piper leading a long line of ragged eco-warriors. There was Birch Daughter, Major Survival, Holly Green and probably the King of the Trees, all looking like they'd been dragged through a hedge backwards. Perhaps they had. Almost all of the protesters had come down from their tree-houses and out of their tunnels – except for those who had concreted themselves into position. Scrag was so surprised that he forgot to bark at the tattered army. The travellers trooped up to the edge of the pitch and chanted and cheered. They distracted the visiting team and before long their passion infected the Panthers. With a few shouted suggestions, Earth Prince soon plugged the leaky defence. "Come on!" he yelled, clapping his hands. "Do you want to lose your last game? Let's see some fight!"

"Yeah," Holly said. "You can get back into this one."

The supporters' cries fired up the forwards and overwhelmed Leasowe Youth who had expected to stroll through the match. Suddenly, Cameron ran on to a long ball. He let it drop over his shoulder and bounce once, then he chipped it over the outstretched arms of the charging keeper. The reds had pulled back one goal and Max held up a celebratory thumb to Adrian. The scruffy supporters responded with an even bigger roar.

Twice Cameron threatened to burst through the defence again and each time, Leasowe's big centre-back stopped him by yanking on his shirt. The crowd cried, "Penalty!" but the ref ignored the appeals. But he couldn't ignore the third foul. It

 **Q:** WHICH TWO BRITISH SIDES SHARE THE NICKNAME THE DONS?

happened right in front of him and Cameron ended up on the ground, his shirt ripped from shoulder to waist. From the spot, the forward blasted the ball into the roof of the net and a new game had begun.

The half-time talk was all about going out with a bang. Even Cameron's spirits were high. "We're gonna win this!" He was also thinking that it would be a great boast if he got a hat-trick against the league-leaders in their final game. When he strode back on to the pitch, determination was written all over his face.

The break also allowed Leasowe Youth to reorganize themselves and recognize that they had a real game on. At the start of the second half, they steadied themselves, got back their shape and composure, and scored a third goal.

The heads of the Panthers began to droop but the travelling supporters lifted the players straight away. "Plenty of time to come back." Then, for thirty minutes, the game became a stalemate. With a few minutes to go, Max unexpectedly received his keeper's sliced drop-kick. He was about to punt it upfield to safety when Earth Prince shouted, "No! You've got space. Use it." Max charged up the wing. At the same time, the coach and Earth Prince called for a midfielder to drop into the hole that he had left.

Finding himself in unfamiliar territory near the opponents' goal-line, Max dummied one defender, looked up and put in a cross. It didn't go to the player Max had singled out. Cameron was not prepared to let it go to anyone else. It was his. He ran in at speed and threw himself at it. His bullet header was past Leasowe's keeper before he could move an inch.

The Panthers should have gone on to win. They nearly did.

Q: WHICH PREMIERSHIP GROUND IS FOUND WITHIN ONE MILE OF LIVERPOOL'S ANFIELD STADIUM?

But it was a game of football and not a fairy tale. At the death of the game, Max found himself racing against Leasowe's sharpest forward for the ball. Against the odds, Max's foot got there first. Even better, the ball came off the Leasowe striker's leg before it trickled over the line. Max's dad signalled a goal kick but the referee overruled him and pointed to the corner flag. Angry, Max cried, "You've got to be joking! No way that ball. . ." Out of the corner of his eye, Max saw Earth Prince place a forefinger across his lips and shake his head. The traveller's expression told him not to argue. Because Max had thought better of protesting, the ref decided not to book him for dissent. But Max could do nothing about the cracking shot that came from the corner. It hit him on the shoulder and deflected high into the goal.

In a glorious defeat, the Panthers went down four-three.

Earth Prince congratulated them as if they'd pulled off a major victory and sympathized with their bad luck. Then he issued a challenge. To mark the end of the club, he offered to scrape together a team of protestors to play a friendly match against Heswall Panthers on Christmas Eve. "It's pretty boring in a protest camp, you know. Until the bailiffs arrive, that is. Then we'll be too busy resisting eviction to play footy."

The Panthers accepted the challenge.

Mr and Mrs Deakin didn't approve but they weren't going to stand in Max's way. After all, his beloved team was about to collapse. But the road contractors did try and stop them. The workers had already erected a tall wire fence right round the ground. When the Panthers saw it, they groaned. The sturdy

Q: WHO IS EUROPE'S MOST CAPPED INTERNATIONAL PLAYER?

barrier was the first undeniable sign that their team had reached the end of the road.

The keeper muttered, "It's really happening. I've been playing for this team since I was nine and now they're taking our pitch!"

"Rotten roads."

"I can't believe it."

"It's tragic."

"What are we going to do now? We can't even have a last friendly."

Some wanted to give up, go home and be miserable over Christmas. Others wanted to climb over the wire but it was impossible. When the eco-warriors arrived, though, Adrian soon sorted it out. He looked at the fence and said, "No problem."

"You must be brilliant climbers."

"No," he replied. "Just good with wire cutters."

One of the Panthers said, "Someone'll see and arrest us or something."

The cold eyes of the silent lorries, parked by the pitch and at the other side of the copse, seemed to be watching. The hungry wagons would not be dormant for long.

Earth Prince smiled. "It's Christmas Eve. No one's working. Believe me, I know contractors and security officers. They'll enjoy their Christmas and then try to surprise us straight after. That's when battle'll commence." He sounded upbeat but there was dread and sadness behind his words.

The ragbag of players filed into the playing area through the hole in the fence. Scrag, being the smallest, went first. He was delighted. While the others mucked around with a ball, he'd investigate his favourite places and his favourite smells.

Q: WHO IS THE LONGEST SERVING ENGLAND MANAGER OF ALL TIME?

Adrian was a star. He went past tackles as if they hadn't been made. His passes were inch perfect, threaded intricately between opposing players. And the grin on his face told everyone he was delighted to be playing again – even in a chaotic kick-about. It was such a pity, Max thought, that he'd dropped football in favour of saving the environment. To make up for Earth Prince, some of his team-mates hadn't got a clue.

Playing against such a mixed bunch was strange. Holly got the first goal. It was Max's fault. She was offside, of course, when she took Adrian's precision pass, but there was no one with a flag to rescue the split defence. Max should have gone in hard and slid the ball away from her but, because she was female, he held back. And she punished him for it. Afterwards, she winked at him. "Bet you're not so polite next time."

No one really knew the score when Max heard Scrag's strange yelp. "Just a minute," he cried and ran towards his dog.

Where the field met the brook, Scrag had dug a deep hole and was backing away from something he'd just picked up in his mouth.

"It's all right, boy," Max said, slapping Scrag's back. Puzzled, Max knelt down by the unmoving lump that Scrag had unearthed. Despite the dog's whimper, Max picked it up. An ugly grey ball with brownish green blisters filled his palm. Its surface was slightly tacky. "What...?"

At his side, Cameron said, "That's a toad, that is. All covered in warts."

A bright yellow stripe extended from the top of its head, between its bulging eyes, to its rear end. The line went right down the middle of its blistered back as if the creature had been

Q: HOW MANY MATCHES DID SCOTLAND WIN WITH ITV LINKMAN BOB WILSON BETWEEN THE POSTS?

marked by a cruel science teacher who was about to slice it precisely into two. "Looks like Scrag found it down a hole but he must have dropped it pretty quick."

"That's coz toads are poisonous."

Curious, Max turned it over. Underneath, the toad was dirty white with deep green blobs. "I think it's dead," he said. "I hope Scrag didn't do it in."

"Nah," Cameron replied. "It's asleep. Don't you pay attention in science? Toads hibernate through the cold. They must be stupid to miss all that footy."

Adrian arrived with a grin and asked, "What you got there?"

"A toad," Max answered, holding it out. "Dead or fast asleep."

At once, Earth Prince became serious. "That's..." He shouted for Birch Daughter by her real name of Beth. She was one of the protestors who lived locally. "Got your mobile? I suggest you call your big brother."

"It's Christmas Eve. He'll kill me."

"This isn't the time to be squeamish. I think these two have got us a natterjack toad."

"So?" Max and Cameron said together.

"If I'm not mistaken, everyone thought they'd died out in these parts – and most other parts of Britain."

"So?"

"Don't you see? If I'm right and there's a colony of them here, no one can touch this place. They're an endangered species, protected by law. You get a whacking great fine for killing them."

Apparently talking into her hand, Beth was persuading her brother, who worked for the Cheshire Wildlife Trust, to get into

Q: WHERE DO ARSENAL PLAY THEIR HOME MATCHES?

his car and speed to the works site. "I wouldn't be calling," she was saying, "if it wasn't important. Yes, it's urgent if you don't want a load of bulldozers to squash flat a family of natterjack toads." She listened to his startled reply and then added, "That's what we reckon they are, yes. OK. See you in a few minutes." Putting the phone away, she announced to the others, "He's on his way."

"Great," Earth Prince said. To Max, he added, "Whatever you do, don't drop the evidence. He might wake up and run off."

The possible find of an ugly natterjack toad was so momentous that Beth's brother brought a friend from English Nature. Together, they examined Max's precious captive and immediately declared that it belonged to an endangered species. Then they bent down by Scrag's hole and peered at the exposed sandy soil. They looked like police officers at the scene of a crime, hunting for tiny clues. When they stood up, they were both smiling. "There's quite a few burrows down there, so there's a substantial colony. This is a superb discovery. We've got to thank you."

Earth Prince waved a hand towards the gathering works traffic. "Just in time."

The men from the conservation groups nodded. "Leave them to us," Beth's brother said with relish. "The Council's going to have to think again. It's illegal to drive a road through a site of special scientific interest." He was looking forward to throwing a weighty spanner into the authority's works. He extracted a camera from his pocket and began to photograph the evidence.

Max said, "You mean we can keep our pitch?"

Q: HOW WAS JUVENTUS MANAGER DINO ZOFF REWARDED FOR WINNING THE ITALIAN CUP AND UEFA CUP IN 1990?

"Courtesy of the toads, yes," the other wildlife expert replied.

Beth's brother added, "As long as you keep your dog away in future." He pointed to the toad still sleeping in Max's hand. "Now, let's take this fellah's portrait then get him back in a burrow and fill the hole in before any more damage is done."

The eco-warriors punched the air. "Yes! Battle won before it even starts!"

Birch Daughter grinned. "I can go home and get a shower at last."

"Yeah," Adrian agreed. "And get your Christmas presents."

"Magic. If I kiss the toad, do you think he'll turn into a handsome prince?"

"Don't try it," Adrian cried. "Princes aren't a protected species. We'd be back to square one."

"What about you, Adrian?" asked Max. "Where's your home?"

Earth Prince shrugged. "Wherever there's the threat of a new road. The new Birmingham motorway, I should think. But..."

"What?"

"I'll hang on here over Christmas. I guess a lot of us will – so we can celebrate in the wood. And I'll see if I can make it to some of your matches next year. I owe you that."

Max nodded. "Yeah. That'd be good."

"Anyway," Earth Prince said, "now we've sorted out one bit of serious business, let's crack on with the other. I didn't hear the final whistle."

"No," Max replied. With a huge grin, he said, "It's still game on."

Max and Cameron led the charge back on to the pitch where

 **Q:** WHICH LEAGUE SIDE ARE KNOWN AS THE GRECIANS?

the others were messing around. The captain's crazy cheers, Cameron's wildly waving arms and Scrag's excited barks told them that Heswall Panthers were still in business. Come the new year, they could begin their long climb back up the league.

Quiz Answers

The Shirt on Your Back

p133 Reading.

p134 Rangers.

p135 A pair of "lucky" white spats he wore throughout the cup run.

p136 Lothar Matthaus.

p137 Barcelona.

p138 Brian Clough. It took him just two hundred and nineteen games.

p139 Bert Trautmann of Manchester City.

p140 Celtic – in 1967.

p141 Four.

p142 None.

p143 Seventeen.

p145 Sir Alf Ramsey.

p146 Gabriel Batistuta.

Dynamite Dave

p151 Aston Villa.

p152 Rene "El Loco" Higuita.

p153 "Big" Ron Atkinson.

p154 Sheffield.

p155 Davor Suker of Croatia.

p156 Sir Stanley Matthews (1956).

p158 Barcelona.

p159 Graham Taylor.

p160 Jurgen Klinsmann of Germany.

p161 None.

p162 Alex Ferguson.

p163 Pelé.

p164 Burnley.

p165 George Weah of Liberia.

p166 Norman "Bite Yer Legs" Hunter.

The End of the Road

p171 Paul Ince.

p172 The Iron.

p173 Just six seconds!

p174 West Bromwich Albion.

p175 None.

p176 Chelsea – hammered by Leeds in the 1967–68 season.

p177 Subbuteo.

p178 Aberdeen and Wimbledon.

p179 Goodison Park. The home of Everton.

p180 Thomas Ravelli of Sweden.

p181 Sir Walter Winterbottom. He endured the hot seat for an incredible 139 games.

p183 None. (Although he did only play twice.)

p184 Highbury Stadium.

p185 He was sacked!

p186 Exeter City.